Praise for Max Besora's *The Adventures and Misadventures of the Extraordinary and Admirable Joan Orpí, Conquistador and Founder of New Catalonia*

"If Cervantes and the Monty Python guys were shoved into the Large Hadron Collider—and Earth didn't explode—we might get something like *Joan Orpí*. How lucky are we to be alive! And to have Max Besora!"
—Ryan Chapman, author of *Riots I Have Known*

"The cod seventeenth-century idiom used by Besora's characters (which he persistently disrupts with contemporary slang) as well as his fondness for arcane words, have all been rendered magnificently into English by Mara Faye Lethem, whose command of the language would seem to know no bounds [. . .] The result is, quite simply, a blast of highly recommendable, unadulterated fun. As Rabelais once said: 'For all your ills, I give you laughter.' Please."
—Matthew Tree, *Times Literary Supplement*

"This raunchy, foulmouthed, and hilarious story brilliantly inhabits the space between novel and biography."—*Publishers Weekly* (Starred Review)

"Flagrant, shameless, high-voltage, and sometimes just consummately silly. I can't think of another translator who could have pulled this off, but like any great writer who feels they have total license to do whatever the hell they want with their language, Lethem creates what the narrator describes as 'a language that constitutes the topography of its own world,' not striving for an accurate period reconstruction, but an archaism that's invented, anachronistic, bastardised, defiantly inconsistent and enormously fun." —Daniel Hahn

**Other Books by Max Besora
in English Translation**

*The Adventures and Misadventures of the Extraordinary and
Admirable Joan Orpi, Conquistador and Founder of New Catalonia*

THE FAKE MUSE

Max Besora

Translated from the Catalan by Mara Faye Lethem

Originally published in Catalan as *La musa fingida* by Editorial Males Herbes S.C.P.

Copyright © 2020 by Max Besora

Published by arrangement with Editorial Males Herbes S.C.P.

Translation copyright © Mara Faye Lethem, 2025

First edition, 2025

All rights reserved

Library of Congress Cataloging-in-Publication Data: Available.

ISBN (pb): 978-1-960385-33-8 | ISBN: (ebook): 978-1-960385-34-5

Cover design by Alban Fischer

Printed on acid-free paper in the United States of America.

Open Letter is the Univeristy of Rochester's nonprofit, literary translation press:
Morey Hall 303, Rochester, NY 14627

www.openletterbooks.org

THE FAKE MUSE

GUEST STARRING

King and Queen Kong

The Bronx Butchers

Manuel, the mutant hamster

"Vampire" Johnny

. . . and many other characters!

Dedicated to . . . . with love.

Signed:
The author (under duress by his characters)

If you seek revenge, dig two graves.
Chinese proverb

TABLE OF CONTENTS

Welcome to the V@lley of the Bronx! 15

Mandyjane Gets Her Revenge 95

The Fake Muse 139

Welcome to the V@lley of the Bronx!

AMANDA

heyyy i'm amanda jane holofernes i'm seventeen and my zodiac sign is scorpio aka brave but

sometimes violent my favorite color is red and i like romance novels because that's as close as i'll get to real love but at the same time it's all really dark

this week my horoscope says the tension between uranus and mars will lead me to put myself in some really annoying situations but that the stars and the planets wont affect my life in the slightest but i'm not so sure

when i'm alone in my room the monster (codename here: ☠☠☠) emerges from the depths of the night and takes off my pajamas with his gummy tentacles and touches me while I look at the reflection of my innocent white skin in his evil eyes

i mean we can all be a bit slutty when we put our minds to it but there's a good bit of difference between slutty and stupid and I can not stand ☠☠☠ when he whips me with his belt on my tits and ass the pig girls like me deserve nice things not nasty stuff like that

it's always the same nightmare and what if you have no story? what if you leave no trace? and what if you are just you standing in that room with all those flowers

yellow ones
> and orange ones
>> and brown ones

i take a selfie smoking an almogavers™ cigarette and upload it to insta

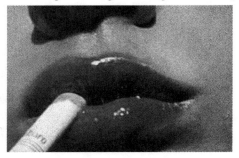

and that reminds me i'm alive   even when I'm sleeping and when I wake up ☠☠☠ is by

my side taking down my panties with his tentacles fucken asshole pervert and that's how it's been for years he comes on moonless nights and takes on different forms like the devil

the difference is that no way am i gonna make a pact with that monster so when ☠☠☠ draws near i'm a crack on the wall

i'm a sharpened knife

i'm a poisonous gas

i'm a world war

I'M THE ONE WHO'LL PUT AN END TO THIS EVIL

sometimes i fantasize about ramming a broomstick up ☠☠☠'s ass—zas!—and filling his mouth with shit and piss tying him up and gagging him and then leaving him like that for three days crying naked with vomit coming out his nostrils

it's that monster's fault i fell into flaming chasms

i descended into the shadows of perversion

i navigated the seven seas and saw whole civilizations die

and now i am standing in my bedroom and ☠☠☠ has me by the tits grabbing me with his tentacles and not letting me open my mouth or move my fingers as he sticks his carnal and cannibal stinger into me and i know that i have no other choice but to go crazy or put lethal poison on my cunt and kill whoever dares to touch me and turn into a merciless and destructive bitch in this room filled with flowers

green ones

and black ones

and purple ones

—are you getting nauseous?—i'm a multitude of viruses enormous sensation of immortality i'd like to think that love moves the world but that's not the truth the truth is that everyone needs attention in this life

i'd say that ☠☠☠ is already approaching because the sun is rotting behind buildings and the wind drags miseries toward the sea and the valley of the bronx is dyed black—i would say that

☠☠☠ is already approaching because i can hear my mother screaming you're a whore one day i'll kill you i'll break that fucking disgusting face of yours the psychopaths are escaping the asylums and the squares fill with innocent victims i would say that ☠☠☠ is already approaching i can hear his tentacles dragging along the hallway and he barks "don't tell anyone"

the silence is resilient   sharpened   precise

some people get lost forever and it's not like i give a shit

i am inside the kingdom of my bed and i want to shout my skin is impure—i scratch it with a knife til i bleed—oh why can't the world be as simple as a sharpened knife?

sometimes i wish i could be like my dog molecule and bark at everybody

sometimes i think i have superpowers i feel like i can walk through walls fly through the sky knock down whole buildings i feel truly enlightened as if i could reach everything between heaven and earth we only search for freedom when we've lost it

and on the other hand i only dream that i dream that i'm lost in a labyrinth   buried   under the bed i have   the mark of slavery tattooed on the twilight of my body the mark left by his tentacles devouring creatures in the night erasing our names oblivion and the friction of bodies increases and the rooster's morning call awakens humanity's libido without the shadow of a doubt

i would say that ☠☠☠ is already approaching because the weddings and funerals multiply and flowers sprout from cracks in cement and there are more traffic accidents than expected

i feel like screaming i'm not your little whore anymore i'm not amanda jane holofernes anymore from now on everyone will know me as mandyjane deathlove and then i will rise up above the sun like an icarus and i will escape the labyrinth filled with ☠☠☠☠☠☠☠☠☠☠☠☠☠☠☠☠☠ ☠☠☠☠☠☠☠☠☠☠☠☠☠☠☠☠☠☠☠☠☠☠☠☠☠☠☠ ☠☠☠☠☠☠☠☠☠☠☠☠☠☠☠☠☠☠☠☠☠☠☠☠☠☠☠ ☠☠☠☠☠☠☠☠☠☠☠☠☠☠☠☠☠☠☠☠☠☠☠☠☠☠☠ ☠☠☠☠☠☠☠☠☠☠☠☠☠☠☠☠☠☠☠☠☠☠☠☠☠☠☠ ☠☠☠☠☠☠☠☠☠☠☠☠☠☠☠☠☠☠☠☠☠☠☠☠☠☠☠ ☠☠☠☠☠☠☠☠☠☠☠☠☠☠☠☠☠☠☠☠☠☠☠☠☠☠☠ ☠☠☠☠☠☠☠☠☠☠☠☠☠☠☠☠☠☠☠☠☠☠☠☠☠☠☠ ☠☠☠☠☠☠☠☠☠☠☠☠☠☠☠☠☠☠☠☠☠☠☠☠☠☠☠ ☠☠☠☠☠☠☠☠☠☠☠☠☠☠☠☠☠☠☠☠☠☠☠☠☠☠☠ ☠☠☠☠☠☠☠☠☠☠☠☠☠☠☠☠☠☠☠☠☠☠☠☠

JOHNNY

my name is joan pons but my friends call me johnny dynamite after some porn actor you know how when they give you a nickname like that it sticks with you for life

i'm thirty-four years old and my zodiac sign is aries i read somewhere that aries are honest but temperamental my favorite color is black and my favorite book is a *thousand vampires* by the writer kim gonzo

the other day i went to the movies with my girl rita rico   it musta been a friday evening like any other friday evening they were showing *nosferatu* by f. w. murnau with subtitles

i've seen *nosferatu* thirty times for real i'm not kidding it's my favorite movie i identify with the atmosphere and the plot and the main character i think the actor max schreck does an incredible job rita wanted to buy popcorn peanut m&ms and cocacola NO i said eat at home or in a restaurant the theater is for watching movies not eating

the theater was empty except for a couple of teenagers who were making out in one corner obviously they weren't there to see *nosferatu*   there was an old hobo who just came to take a nap and was already snoring before the coming attractions started as if his life was escaping from his esophagus there is nothing grosser than listening to somebody snoring in a movie theater unless someone comes

unless someone comes in just as the movie's starting SITS RIGHT IN FRONT OF YOU it's not like there aren't any other empty seats i say to rita and the dude has to sit here what a yobbo and it wasn't just that his big balloon head blocked half the screen and he had a huge bucket of popcorn and he started chewing and slurping cocacola or whatever it was that

he was slurping can ya believe the noise this pig sitting here is making i say to rita rico but she says shit man chill out güey don't be garrapatero watch the movie and relax and later we'll go hang out and have some dinner and then we'll go out and do some serious bumpin and grindin on the dance floor perrea, perrea come on wey focus on the screen juanito don't freak out she tells me as

if it wuz that easy that fuckin gross pig keeps on making noise right when the credits are starting and i'm getting more and more nervous and i can't believe i forgot my valiums at home gottdamn there is nothing that gets under my skin more than the sound of a

mouth frenetically chewing popcorn in fact that shit is much worse than a dying old dude's snoring oh dear nosferatu have pity on all these bastards did you notice? i say to

my bae after a few minutes i think he's doing it on purpose i say to rita nobody slurps cocacola like that he's doing it on purpose the fucken summabitch

come on weyyyy simmer down says rita stop it already with your pendejadas it's like something out of a b-movie or a z-movie you're like a little kid . . . by the way remind me to pack you a lunch for tomorrow k?

a spasm runs up my spine like a boa constrictor i couldn't stand the lunches rita rico packed for me cuz they were like the ones my mother made me to take to

school i just couldn't stand those lunches i couldn't stand them i hated having to carry them around all the time those two or three greasy plastic containers it was horrible and now rita rico does the same thing the exact same thing that my moms used to do

she spends the whole damn day making lunches to put in tupperware rita rico turned into my mother it's a horrible feeling i look into her eyes and i see my mother with that look my mother had when she was about to fill up some tupperware she has the same gleam in her eyes like she's about to pack a damn lunch

i can't stand food i watch the rats on the street eating trash and i want to eat the rats and garbage   my teeth look like sevillian castanets max schreck the actor who plays nosferatu fills the enormous screen and the fat pig in front of me won't stop chewing and swallowing and it all feels like some terrible joke in a monochromatic landscape

i even take a photo of the movie screen to remember the vampire's elegant figure and i upload it to snapchat immediately

i was trying to concentrate on the movie but between us and the enormous screen were the horrible noises that disgusting guy in front of us was making with his popcorn prolly was the typical obese spoiled brat forty years old and still living with his mommy   one of those losers who've never worked a day in his life and collects star wars figures

one of those losers who has every possible allergy known to science because they can't stomach their shitty lives and their mother is so overprotective she treats em like retards or embryos in jars filled with uterine liquid and ended up creating some sort of monster who can't do shit but thinks he's got the right to walk around like a little dictator

overprotected dudes that bug you with conversations so stupid and banal that you want to puke on yourself or run away   the kind of people the world does not need

you know the kind of person i'm talking bout right? i say to my bae overpopulation of these maniacal spoiled brats somebody oughta do something don't you think? i say to rita deport them to the antarctic or some far-off desolate cold place so they wise up

but sooner or later they'd end up coming back so best to just eliminate them once and for all i say to rita órale shut the fuck up bueeeyyyy she says to me she doesn't understand my position but i can't stand another second the fat disgusting spoiled slob making a horrific sound in front of me all i could see was his round head and i hated him and his popfuckingcorn

i felt like smashing something i wanted to i really wanted to

suddenly   i got up from my seat and ran out of the theater and ran to the toilets

i looked in the mirror i was all sweaty and pale when i opened my mouth i saw that two massive fangs were growing in my gums my face had turned super white like the living dead

i backed up scared

slowly slowly my body was getting blurry and disappearing from the mirror

and suddenly i had a terrific desire to bite something something alive to sink my teeth into something human

i was all TERRIBLY VAMPIRIZED

i ran into the darkness of the theater rita was screaming where you going pendejo? ándale pinche puto no te hagas nalga . . . man don't get all cantiflas on me . . . no seas tan denso carnal you know eso de la movida . . . you know how it is ándale cabrón but i walked past my bae without even listening to her and i leapt over the seat and landed in one right in front of ours and i opened my mouth in the direction of

the neck of that mental retard who was still eating fucken popcorn making a horrible sound   i bit i chewed up the neck of that gross guy sinking my teeth in again and again and without stopping over and over as the schlub had less and less neck and i felt his hot blood in my mouth

the popcorn went flying and the guy had no ears and barely any face and no neck left tearing off bites of his face was the only option i had in that particular moment because deep down that

disgusting man was no longer real i mean he wasn't important he was just a shadow in the shadows there was no difference between me and nosferatu and that doesn't mean a thing it means nothing to me i don't mean next to nothing it does not mea

MERITXELL

hey what's up i'm meritxell hernández my zodiac sign is leo and leos are passionate but obstinate this week my horoscope says that excessive honesty could screw up my relationships

my favorite color is red i work as a professional model first of all i want to clear something up most people   think i'm an idiot just because i'm so pretty and tall that's because normally everybody's stuck on a series of clichés that are super hard to change for example people assume that all models are as idiotic as we are pretty or that all feminists hate men or that all environmentalists are liberals who come from money

but all that stuff is just stereotypes there's nothing more toxic than a stereotype i have a degree in biology a masters in environmental sciences and i'm a member of the radical ecological group earth first! i think that what we humans do to animals and the planet's resources and atmosphere is basically just

mass suicide   we humans are the apocalypse that's the honest truth and believe me i've thought about it more than two or three times

but people who don't know me always see me as a mental retard just because i work as a model and all the boyfriends i've had just wanted me for sex and to show me off to their friends like i'm some sort of swimming trophy or a blow-up doll THE WORLD IS FULL OF ASSHOLES

    the other day my friend trini gave me a present so i wouldn't feel so alone she told me i have a surprise for you because now that you finally dumped your stupid boyfriend you need some company   when i opened up the little box i found a hamster

that little animal was so cute and i IMMEDIATELY took a photo with my phone and i uploaded it to insta but then i said to my friend

    thank you so much trini but i can't accept pet trafficking i don't want to participate in or perpetuate animal abuse

    i mean look at bullfighting look at the zoo in the valley of the bronx the animals there have terrible lives the buffalos are mangy the penguins' eyes are falling out of their sockets and what about the pharmaceutical industry experimenting on animals destroying chimpanzees' brains to see if they can count to 3

    and also im fucking fed up with everybody taking pictures with kittens or photos swimming with dolphins and sea turtles and after they put them up on social media they eat an industrial hamburger without blinking an eyelash it's like we're all retarded

    come on shut up says trini don't start with your sermons my friend told me its a syrian golden hamster that an animal rights association saved from from the university of saint jeremias the laboratory students were able to establish unbelievable neuronal connections inside its little brain this hamster is special said trini it quotes famous dead writers and anyway i can't give it back to the animal rights association it's not like buying a fucking tee shirt you know? besides look how cute the hamster is look how it talks look

Some books are to be tasted, others to be swallowed, and some few to be chewed and digested.
Sir Francis Bacon

it was a very sophisticated and well-read hamster in the end i decided to keep it what name should i give it i asked my model friend its scientific name is *cricetus auratus* but call it MANUEL i think this hamster looks like a MANUEL okay i said and

ever since then manuel lives with me i feed him i take care of him i watch how he spins around on his little wheel for hours like a bat outta hell and then i get on my stationary bike to do my spinning we're both so happy pedalling i say good morning manuel and he says stuff to me like

Read and you will lead, don't read and you shall be lead.
Saint Teresa of Ávila

we pedal and pedal and pedal as if we were both reaching some altered state of consciousness as if i and my hamster could communicate on a higher level through pedalling

the other day i saw that manuel was shivering cold in his cage and i had an idea i thought the microwave might be a bit warm anyway i put manuel in there while he said to me

Words are all we have.
Samuel Beckett

the next day when i went to take him out of the microwave he was acting really strange trembling and his eyes were all red and bloodshot and he was puking up a really gross white liquid so i decided to take him to the vet but the vet said i don't know what's wrong with him the best thing would be to put him down manuel got scared and said

> *The time will come when men such as I will look upon the murder of animals as they now look upon the murder of men.*
> **Leonardo da Vinci**

no way i said to the vet because i'm against killing animals and abuse . . .

up to you goodbye said the vet without even letting me finish what i was saying and then I was charged a fucking huge bill

i took manuel home i put him in his cage and he didn't want to eat any of the stuff i gave him i fell asleep all worried and all i could hear was him quoting famous writers nonstop it was horrible

> *We can judge the heart of a man by his treatment of animals.*
> **Immanuel Kant**

the next morning i was awoken by a very loud noise and i realized that my bedroom no longer existed and i was in the middle of the street there were people everywhere what is going on i asked a fireman a monster destroyed your building there it is look

i looked toward where the fireman was pointing and none other than manuel he'd grown thirty meters and there he was destroying all those buildings he just wanted to be free but soon the army showed up with their tanks and planes to bomb him while he shot laser rays out of his eyes

the tv news captured the moment in a horrific image

> *As long as there are slaughterhouses,*
> *there will always be battlefields*
> **Leo Tolstoy**

don't put up a fight manuel i shouted to him i'm begging you please   let's go i ordered let's run away together

the mutant hamster put me up on his disgustingly hairy back and we traveled three hundred kilometers in less than an hour fleeing the tanks and the police far far away from the valley of the bronx

we took refuge in some remote mountains in the valley of cold springs and we built a nest far from the maddening world isn't it great we'll live here you and me what do you say to that? i asked him and he said to me

> *Love is a beautiful flower,*
> *but we must be brave enough to pick her up*
> *from the edge of a precipice.*
> **Stendhal**

the radiation from the microwave had made manuel's brain grow exponentially in conjunction with his gigantic body now he could not only quote authors but create complex mathematical formulas and at the same time think of what to make for lunch he was a genius

manuel started writing a book titled *tractatus logico rodentia* a rigorous study on the false truths of humankind designed to emancipate all rodents and animals in general from human servitude i took dictation of what he said as fast as i could into my moleskine notebooks

our life there together was perfect the days slid by and my feelings for manuel grew more and more special it wasn't exactly his looks that attracted me but his self-confidence and his privileged intellect which i'd never seen before in any human not even a college professor

one night when he was dictating a part of his book our mouths drew close and we kissed oh my god it was incredible to feel his rodent teeth and his giant rough tongue inside my mouth then we sought out neutral ground and we made

love all night long it was very romantic in two weeks we had a 50,000-page doctoral thesis of his *tractatus*:

> [. . .] first it was religion and then technology, among other things, that created the modern concept of speciesism, which supposes that animals do not have a right to life or freedom. Human beings believe they have the power to decide when an animal or a plant dies but they do not realize that humankind is just another species, an animal, a mammal, a product of nature. I proclaim the end of their reign of moral superiority. Ecofuturism is now a reality because I think like a hamster, therefore I am a hamster. I assert that the human cogito has been programmed for obsolence because it has just been overtaken. And that is the final word on that (Manuel, 2095: 7)

that was the general tone of the thesis which we sent to a small independent publisher it was a bestseller in the human population thanks to word of mouth it was immediately translated into three hundred languages including swahili and braille television crews and dedicated journalists showed up every day in helicopters to interview the famous mutant hamster

academia and the publishing world in general wrote rave reviews of the book like the prestigious senior professor at the university of saint jeremias walter colloni in the journal *the new pork review* which i quote here:

> With his *Tractatus Logico Rodentia*, Manuel the hamster erects a framework to sustain the ecofuturist theories that, in turn, will form the basis of the subversive reading of works written by all sorts of animals. The creation and composition of these works will transform the established norm of the evolution of animal and vegetable species, and revolutionize the later canonical movements, etc.

top-tier intellectuals called for him to be awarded the nobel prize for the originality of his *tractatus* i mean who's ever heard of a hamster writing philosophical treatises? a gossip magazine asked me how i could have fallen in love with a mutant hamster love is more than skin deep i answered i'm not looking for guys with big pecs who spend their days at the gym taking selfies i prefer a brilliant mind . . . and the giant cock is a big plus too hahahahahahaha!

we were invited to international social events and even to the white house where we were received by none other than the president of the united states our lives took a 180^0 turn money did grow on trees someone gifted us a victorian mansion in london and we even had a destination wedding in rome we rubbed elbows with

famous writers and actors and we lived seriously large we had no more private life the paparazzi took turns trying to snag a photo of manuel taking out the garbage or shopping for groceries for example

extremist religious organizations camped out in front of our house to protest with signs demanding capital punishment for that aberration of a hamster while other animal rights associations like earth first! or animal front liberation showed their support but criticized us for having become so bourgeois and living a life so distanced from the original precepts of his *tractatus logico rodentia*

soon all that social pressure and falling in with the wrong crowd meant manuel was doing cocaine and ketamine he spent his nights at the clubs with his lovers he became aloof and we hardly ever made love anymore but even still i

got pregnant and i had an abortion at an illegal clinic in brazil because i didn't want my child to grow up in that toxic atmosphere before throwing the fetus into the trash i looked at it and confirmed that such a hybrid of human and hamster would never be accepted by society (or even by me because it was really disgusting)

when manuel found out he beat the crap out of me scratching my face with his claws you're a misogynistic territorial abuser if you'd worn a condom none of this would've happened i shouted at him shut up he said baring his rodent teeth you're a murderer that was your own child even if it wasn't human and couldn't speak and he added

The question is not, Can they reason?
Nor, Can they talk?
But, Can they suffer?
Jeremy Bentham

you can stuff your quotations where the sun don't shine i don't give two shits about your intellectual reflections you've changed manuel you're nuts i don't know you anymore fame has gone to your head what happened to your desire to change the world to subvert the prevailing values

don't you realize you've merely gone from living in a hamster cage to living in a human cage with lots of cable tv channels?

after that speech it seemed like manuel was coming to his senses he admitted that focusing on his academic theories while writing his *tractatus* had distanced him completely from mundane problems and he suspected that the supposed neutrality of his book was a fiction designed to only appeal to humans

but what about the animals that don't even know how to read?   manuel wanted to go back to the basics of his own existence and give the animal kingdom the same superpowers he had and not only that manuel explained he had a plan and this was it:

put an end to the reign of humankind on this planet and begin the rule of animalkind the time for academic theorizing was over it was time to for praxis

The wise man does not teach with words but with actions.
Lao Tse

manuel disappeared one night and the next day i found out he was spreading his revolutionary dogma throughout the entire animal kingdom soon strange things started happening all over the world:

a lap dog bit off the nose of his owner with no warning and then sent letters to *the bronx messenger* taking responsibility for the crime:

> *Mrs. Holofernes had to suffer.*
> *There will be more.*
>
> *Signed: "Big Mo"*

the dolphins in an australian zoo chopped up their personal trainer during a televised show

the dairy cows in a farm in bordeaux suddenly organized to devour their farmer overlords to the cry of "who's the hamburger now, bitches!"

bears wolves and deer came down from the mountains in canada to exterminate townspeople

some monkeys bit some ethnologists on the african savannah according to the magic world of the internet stray cats from various overpopulated cities in china ganged up and used their claws and fangs to attack children and eat them

in new barcelona millions of cockroaches and other insects crawled into people's mouths as they slept and choked them to death   urban pigeons freed canaries and other bird species from their cages and flew over the cities pecking out the eyes of pedestrians and they even learned how to steal and drop bombs from the air

whales capsized boats out on the open sea while sharks attacked sunbathers on the beaches the revolution was underway and it was all pretty unpleasant

the united nations and armies all over the world had to intervene it was total war against the animal world

i soon realized that it was all manuel's fault in fact it was caused by my love for animals and if i didn't do something it would lead to the annihilation of my own species i hired a private detective to find manuel he finally told me that the mutant hamster had taken over a nuclear power plant in france with a hundred other animals   so i drove my electric car there as fast as i could

BRAAAMMBBBRRAAAMMRRAAMMM

i got out of the car while it was still running and there was manuel indoctrinating his army with his usual pedantic quotes

The harm that is done to a man should be so serious that one does not stand in fear of revenge.
Niccolò Machiavelli

what the fuck do you think you're doing i asked him and he told me get out of here meritxell this is no place for you this is a matter for animals not humans so butt out

sorry but i'm still your wife and until i see some divorce papers you owe me an explanation the fact is manuel was planning to create a   new race of mutant animals to conquer the planet earth we will destroy all humans he said we will rule the world again we'll kill all these sons of bitches

just like i turned enormous and intellectually gifted via the electromagnetic microwaves with this atomic power i can convert hundreds of animals into mutants like me in ten minutes he said

you've lost your marbles you haven't got a fucking clue about atomic energy i said your case is an exception can't you see that YOU'RE AN ANOMALY

shut the fuck up manuel said you're the anomaly you hamster-fucking bitch you perverted nutbag   i'll show you that with more radiation i can become invincible and then watch out for the   wolves and spiders and chameleons they'll all have mutant superpowers we won't discriminate on the basis of race or of gender or of age not like you humans   you racist homophobes and authoritarians didn't you want animal equality? well here it comes bitch   didn't you want to save the planet earth? well the first step is putting the kibosh on your two-legged egomaniacal race with your moral anthropocentrism

> *I have a question that sometimes drives me hazy:*
> *Am I or the others crazy?*
> **Albert Einstein**

manuel went into the chamber filled with atomic radiation while the other animals watched him with their tongues hanging out and the army arrived with their tanks and planes

i begged pleaded demanded ordered insisted that he please get out of there but it was already too late a shower of radiation fell on him and made all the power plant's sensors reach their maximum readings until finally the entire plant exploded

the animals and the army of soldiers died instantly and the explosion unleashed massive radiation that polluted the air and water on the entire continent but somehow I survived

when i was about to leave i heard a tiny voice from down below

> *When a man has pity on all living creatures*
> *then only is he noble*
> **Buddha**

it was manuel he'd also survived the radiation but instead of making him invincible it had turned him back into his original normal hamster form just four centimeters i couldn't help but laugh wahahahahahahahahahahaha!

i'm so friggin tired of your pedantic bullshit always quoting intellectuals i don't know who the hell you think you are you're nothing more than a hamster with a huge inferiority complex i said lifting up my foot and stomping on his little head with my shoe until his brains came out his mouth

then i picked up his little corpse and like the good environmentalist i am i threw that hamster into the organic waste recycling bin

The only thing you can't recycle is wasted time
Anonymous

JAVIER

my name's javier holofernes i'm fifty-five and my zodiacal sign is virgo virgos are hardworking but very critical of ourselves and others my favorite color is

yellow and my number one book is *how to become a leader in less than 24h* and that's why i'm also the manager of the steel factory in a nearby town called saint pancras of paradise

i live in a villa with a pool in the residential area of the valley of the bronx with my family i go to the gym three days a week to do cardio-bodypump and swimming and i also play tennis once a week with the partners in my company i believe in capitalistic logic i mean that for

example if we didn't have that system what would we have? communism? in a communist system there wouldn't be any tennis clubs and i wouldn't be able to buy a mercedes benz and we would all be slaves to the regime no way could i put up with that i've been married for twenty years with my wife leonor in catholic and apostolic matrimony and we have two daughters amanda and isabel II and an adopted dog named molecule

i vote for a conservative party i won't say which one but they are the only ones i trust because they still believe family values and morals are the guarantees of decency and good taste and they are the only ones who believe in law and order

i mean the violence and brutality that reap terror on the earth know no limits every day you hear about massacres exterminations disappearances and genocides on the tv news the bible already told us that the final days of this world would be filled with cruelty and attacks by one group against another (2 timothy 3:1-5)

i mean look at all the fat people look at the students and the workers look at the immigrants look at the politicians everyone posts their miserable lives on the internet for all to see i call that pornography hard core everyone needs constant attention every level of desperation leads to the flames look at the

friggin horizon of expectations look how all the realities you thought were tangible start to blur and expand look at the murderers look at the thieves look at the bureaucrats everyone everybody's rushing to get somewhere

people get on and off the buses as if they had to do something terribly important but really they can't do anything more than live in their selfish bubble forever those are the real "criminals" but i know that god's fury will send his

army of exterminating angels down from heaven to put an end to all that every sunday i go to mass with my wife and my daughters who i've raised under the precepts of the apostolic roman catholic faith so they will be decent people

in the face of the social and economic changes of society with industrialization and massification of traditional power transforming into an alarming lack of values the world is full of violence and makes no sense and what we need more than ever today are VALUES AND FAITH that is what the priests at my boarding school taught me i remember that

as a kid we would go camping with the priests and they showed us how to make fires and built cabins and love each other i remember father colom one night called me into his tent and when i got there he had his pants and underwear down and he told me come here my son put this

in your mouth if you want to be saved by our lord on the day of final judgment and remove satan from your body put it in your mouth because "so is my word that goes out from my mouth: It will not return to me empty, but will accomplish what I desire and achieve the purpose for which I sent it" (isaiah 55:11)

and so i did it i sucked the old stunted cock of father colom until he started to tremble and finally an explosion of white salty liquid filled my mouth "swallow it my son swallow this divine gift and fulfill the LORD'S DESIGNS" and even though I

tried to swallow it all just like the priest told me there was too much liquid and it dripped from my lips with the priests i learned to obey god's mandate and to have discipline over my body and others' bodies

the world ended in 1914 when satan was thrown from the sky to the earth and that was how the first world war started (apocalypsis 6:4 matthew 24:7 apocalypsis 12:9-12) and since then hell is in our backyard i can hear the screams of the victims on television dead innocent absurd happily god will put an end to all this savagery no more bombs terrorist attacks crimes all that will be a thing of the past (psalms 37:9-11, 29)

that's why i think it's important to save the world from satan just like father colom taught me and that is what I teach my daughters because it's important to continue traditions so we don't lose the little decency and morality left in this world

but sometimes children don't turn out exactly the way you'd hoped they would my younger daughter isabel is still young and does everything we tell her to but the older one amanda doesn't want to even hear about going to mass she started listening to devil music and goes around dressed all in black i think she has satan inside her if i don't do something she will end up falling into evil my wife is incapable of raising anyone that whore is only good for giving pedicures and reading your horoscope i ask for help from the god almighty to give me strength and help me discipline my daughter just like father colom did me

but it's not as easy as it looks to carry out this education it has to be secret evil knows a thousand ways to defeat you and humiliate you on moonless nights satan is invoked and that is when i have to do the exorcism

i go into my daughter's room and make her drink a glass of chocolate milk with diazepam in it so she will relax the drug takes effect i take off her pajamas and i tell her don't speak don't say anything while i try to take satan out of you through your vagina don't speak i tell her shut up and drink the chocolate milk don't say anything don't say

as i touch my daughter i can't stop thinking about the priests and father colom and his rancid cock it's not that i liked the sweet and sour smell of his sweaty cock or licking his hairy balls but it was my duty to take satan out from inside him it was my moral obligation i also think it is a good experience to swallow the

semen of a holy man like father colom even though i wanted to vomit "that liquid will give you strength to fight against evil" he always said in those dark rooms at the boarding school father colom's semen didn't have a color or taste that was particularly different or special compared to the other priests at the school

while i think about all that i lay down beside my daughter after ejaculating i think that for today satan has left her body life is so limited and it is not hard to measure the moral value of things my sight grows blurry my throbbing heart pumps blood to my retinas everything is

dark and only the streetlights illuminate my hopes i imagine father colom crying my mind is confused my daughter doesn't look me in the eye

then i go back to my room i put on my pajamas and my wife who is reading the horoscope says "do you love me?" that simple question sends me into a rage and i shout you are   a bitch i'll break your fucking shitty face ya fucking nutjob i'll punch you so many times not even your own fucking mother will recognize you you don't have the balls she says you don't have the balls to hit me you are

a cowardly bastard all you do is abuse kids fucking faggot son of a motherfu

but i'm not listening anymore i'm sleeping like a baby we are a happy family tomorrow is christmas there are tons of gifts under the tree just like tradition calls for and traditions should be respected

before i go to sleep i take a photo of our christmas tree and i post it on the company's instagram

ISABEL II

hay im isabel holofernes imb thirdeen yeers old and my favrit culla is wite and my favrite brand of klose is calbin clein my horrorscop sine is libra mom always sez that libras r sociaple but kinda insecure but i

dont care wut my mudder saez i hate her and my fadder hes a monster i only love my sister amanda even doe shes cookoo batsy

i like trap dance hall reaggeton every satterday nite we go to the club to shake it shake it with ar freinds and there arr always idiits hoo say shit like "wax yer armpit slag" omg wut a assehorl i dont give a rats

i'm in lurve wit a boi from school his name is marc he drivs me hornt   but i dondare talk to him cuz he's one of the bezlooking guis at the school wut can ya do it wuld be ridickulus that

suddenle i start talking to him cuzz he's always goin after da hottes girls in the school marc muss NOT EBEN NO I EGGSISS i muss seem so pathedick allways stareing at him lik an imbesil but the truth is i coodna care lest fuck im cuz

now i have the latess cyborg 6.0 smartphone wid a 7.7 Hd screen 190 GB memory 2.8 internal processor 15PM camra my new fone has a ton of hilee reckamended applicashuns and takes incredible fotos i take fotoes swimmin with tortusses and dolfins and sexy selfees with my slutte miniscirt showin lotsa legg and i post them on instagram i have 8,000 followrs i want to becum an influenser

wid this telafon and all the "likes" watt do i need a boifriene for? i think that A PERSON WITHOUT SOSHUL MEDIA IS A DED PERSON

but i mosly uz the telafone fer chatding i chat with mi friends from school and also i go evrry day into dadeing apps and all that stuf wen im in my room i go to one of dose sites this is my profil

> Looking for: FRIENDS
> About me: LA, LA, LA
> Proudly single.
> No pervs, pigs or creeps

but gyes rite me nasty stuf anyways and sen me fotoes of their coks i cant help it i get an ego booost from stuf like this

> ey pretty girrrl how you doin? whats yr
> favorit color? btw heres some fotos of my DIKK

or this

> hottie i'd fuck u rite now
> i'm into anal BDSM

and this

> goood mornin: i peerced my nipples and put in two rings and now i can feel the air passing threw my nipples in the summertime and i feel fresh and really good i have a percing on the tip of my knob too heres a photo

stuff like that i udderstand in the magic whorld of the innernet you discober that we're all lonly and that WE ALL WANNA BE LOVED IN A WORL THAT HATES US SO MUSH when i'm not chadding i really do miss them all idon no there real names but ttheir so adorable and frajil

i'm very happy with my noo fhone and its applicashuns i love the coler of my noo telefone its white-black-gold with an impressif imatge qwality thanks to its 7.7 quad HD (2378 X 2330 PX) i enjoy all the colerrs better than ever with 4 times the HD resolushon ultraligth metallic dizine

i'm todtally addicket to chatding and i think i'm fallin in love with a guy on the chat one day he slipt into my dms and sed

> i like girls with greene eyes

i tole him

> what a coincidunce mine are green

my chat handle is "irritable colon"

his was "Marquis de Sade 3000"

since i had nothin to lose we started to chat every day i like the romantic things he rote me and i wood always send him millions of emogees ☺☺☺

> i wanna lick your ass and eat your shit

and

> i want to fuk u in a superstore and cut one of yore nipples with prooning shears in the garden secktion

who woodn't fall for somebody who tells u such priddy things? u cant put anee limits on luv

im so lukky mi noo fone has a specktackular camara with improoved laser autofokus duel flash 500 MAH battree weed bin chatting fer for weeks and it was like i'd nown "Marquis de Sade 3000" forevah   like sumhow we'd met in another life as if it was fayt or sumpin like that had brawt us together

"Marquis de Sade 3000" was so sensitif he confesst his privit secrits to me

> i like to torture animals specially turdles
> and hamsters and alzo i like to burn frogs
> with a ligter

> me too

i wood tell him

i think its importan wen you meet somebuddy with so mutx in commun deez things don happun erry day

one day he tole me his plans for the fyuchure

> I want you to come over i've been thinkin
> about suiside but first i want to eat you so
> we'll be together in death

that was the best decklarashun of lov i ever herd

we have a fyucher together

a whorizun of exspectashuns busting with eturnity and lovv

> i want to start bye cutting off my arm and eat-
> ing it with you then i'll cut off my cock and we'll
> eat it wile we watch a netflix cerial killer show.
> sendin you my leff arm as proof i'm serius
> I LOVE YOU

this is a hi-def foto of his arrm thanks to my state of the art smartphone one day i got a rinkled packig all coverd in rottin blud his arm waz inside

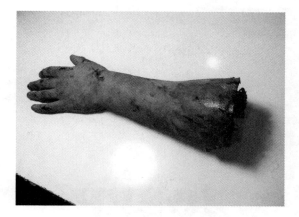

it was the definitif prufe of his love i hid it in the closit in my room for a wile the packidg stunkt like deth but it was my luvvers arm

but one day wenn my father was liing on my side of the bed talkin bout gettin satan out of my boddy and all that he smelt sumthing nazty and he fownd the arm all hurrified

he called the copz and that wuz the end of my chadding with "Marquis de Sade 3000" now the chat is a lonly place

and lovv is sooooo cumplicated

JOSEP

my name is josep antoni but everybody calls me by my alias the kingkong of the bronx and now i'll explain why i'm thirty five and my horoscope is cancer we

cancers are imaginative but temperamental my favorite color is white i work as a chemist in a pharmaceutical lab doing experiments and testing on animals to develop new drugs and they pay me a ton of cheddar for it

but money's not everything in this life i'm bald too alopecia isn't a disease i mean it's not like being an albino having spina bifida or psoriasis alopecia IT'S JUST SHIT LUCK i mean they've invented spaceships . . . we've been to the moon . . . and they still haven't figured out how to grow hair? come on man

people look at you and they don't say anything but i know that inside they're thinking look at that guy he has no hair he must have terminal cancer i can't stand to look at him he must not get any matches on tinder they must think what a ping-pong ball it really sucks let me tell you

and the jokers who say that bald guys are more sexually potent i'd like to rip their heads off what a stupid thing to say a useless myth like the myth that people named josep antoni are good people my friends are always saying you're a good guy josep antoni and for example they say dang josep antoni is a real stand-up guy and my female friends say you're a good boy josep antoni i really like you you're so nice always the same old shit

they think i'm blind or an idiot i'd rather they just told it to me straight that they looked me in the eyes and said fuck you're really bald josep antoni you look like a fucking ping-pong ball

that way i could tell them i don't like your face either i don't know how much you make but i'd recommend an iridectomy or a blepharoplasty to change it they can really do miracles these days with surgery they can change your whole fucking face in any illegal clinic in brazil you idiot

one day i went to my regular supermarket to buy shampoo and a copy of the local newspaper *the bronx messenger* so i could stay current and they'd just changed the cashier it was a totally different cashier it wasn't the same person a charming girl who helped me with a charming smile i said hello how are you you don't

know me but i come here every day to shop i'm a regular customer and first of all i'd like to show you my bald head i said taking off my cap to see what you think and i showed it to her and the cashier stared at it for about ten seconds with a pleasant smile as she scanned the products she seemed really interested

and after i paid with my debit card and i put the shampoo and the newspaper in my cloth bag she said no big deal nobody's perfect you're bald like a ping-pong ball and i don't have arms my name is clàudia by the way

i hadn't noticed but it was true instead of arms the cashier had two wrinkled stumps and she was hitting the register keys with those protrusions of rotted flesh honestly it was kind of disgusting

i'm a member of the association of armless painters if you write down your address i'll send you some really cool christmas postcards with our paintings on them ok that's really interesting i said to her

yeah she said in the painting class they taught me bigger is better . . . in paintbrushes i mean hahaha that allows me to grip better with my feet i think even a person with no arms can live a normal life not only did clàudia have a sense of humor but she was honest too while she was talking all i could see were those stumps those pieces of flesh i observed them with a mix of vomit and perplexity as if nothing else existed

when i left the supermarket i ran home shouting her name in the street clàudia clàudia clàudia

i was in love

for the first time ever i was excited with this infinite love i was feeling for clàudia but i was still really worried about my baldness and every day i went to the supermarket but i never dared to confess my love to her

to solve this problem i started secretly developing a formula in the lab at work after much testing with experimental drugs and human and animal cadavers i finally managed to design a formula made of african rhinoceros and human excrements electricity and industrial liters of rat semen

i was my own guinea pig i took a dose of that steaming blue liquid and i started convulsing and then lost consciousness

when i woke up i looked at my hands they had grown and were covered in dark thick fur my sense of smell and hearing had increased exponentially i looked

into the mirror and saw the reflection of a mass of fur in fact it was much more than that i'd turned into some kind of gorilla and i was making these grunting sounds without wanting to uh-uh!

with all this new hair i am a new man i feel able to confess my love to clàudia the supermarket cashier when she sees me so hairy she will fall in love with me instantly today it's in to be hairy beards and things like that are in and the city is now filled with frigging hipster salons where they charge you

thirty bucks to trim your beard i'm sure that with my new gorilla hair i'm immune to scissors i'm invincible i'm hairily untouchable in the end i've made up my mind and with my new hair i went to the supermarket where clàudia works and i bought a shampoo with conditioner and a classic of neocatalan literature *uncertain ejaculatory* by john sales about some war i don't give a shit about the book it's just an excuse to go to the register and see clàudia

when i get on the line to pay my heart starts beating faster and faster there are three people in front of me waiting when they see me they open their mouths very wide and then shriek in terror involuntarily i start to make guttural sounds uh-uh . . . uh-huh . . . and they all run off leaving their consumer products

it's for the best patience isn't my forte i'm nervous my hands are sweating with all that hair i'm sweating all over goddamnit uh-uh

everyone ran off except for clàudia she's still there organizing the plastic bags with her amputated arms and when i see her i can't help noticing an ascendant inclination between my legs because of the magic formula i developed to grow hair my

testosterone levels are through the roof and my sexual potency is unstoppable I JUST WANT TO COPULATE EXPLOSIVELY day and night uh-uh! and i have alarming priapism no trousers can hide that's why i need to possess clàudia now or i will explode with semen

i go over to the register to pay for the book she says hello: cash or credit and as if she didn't remember who i was with my new fur but i knew that she has a great sense of irony those words of hers and her neutral attitude were a metaphor actually she was telling me you're a freak a monster like me but i will treat you as humanely as possible somehow she was confessing her unconditional love in encrypted code

that made me feel really happy uh-uh! and i ripped up the book in front of her and leaping over the register i told her the truth i said i love you clàudia and i want to go to new york with you i want to go to the u-s-a like king kong and grab you by the hair and climb the empire state building but in the elevator i don't want airplanes shooting at us or policemen arresting us at jfk airport

i want to go to new york like king kong and chase you down fifth ave wondering if your carpet matches your drapes follow you to the brooklyn bridge and beyond i want to go to new york like king kong with you to shout uh-uh! and scare a thousand people at the same time or separately on the stages of broadway (the hard way)

i want us to go from branch to branch like tarzan carries jane i want new york and with each step we'll sink manhattan a little more under the ocean ohpleasemydear i want to go to new york with you like king kong and be a monster with massive fangs an enormous monkey covered in

fleas and ticks in central park and live out a story of love and passion something out of a soap opera you and i together as if we'd totally gone off the grid and with each step the bronx

sinks a little more i want to go to new york like king kong i want to be a monster with foam between my lips on wall street like king kong and go to new york climb the empire state building with you but in the elevator

clàudia smiles with excitement i leap over the register and grab her by her amputated arms and she shouts with happiness and emotion i carry her on my back and we leap through the streets people shriek with terror police sirens are heard in the distance everyone is screaming while i roar uh-uh! and i carry clàudia far from there only love can cause that kind of miracle you know what i mean

now we live in hiding from the law and clàudia asked me to administer the magic formula to her as well she wants to be a queen kong she wants to be hairy she wants to be all hormonal since then we live together hidden from the authorities two monsters like us we'll never fit in with society and its

standards of beauty and we rob banks to pay the bills in this selfie it's me hugging clàudia the day we confessed our love to each other and i just posted it on instagram i'm expecting a lot of "likes"

LEONOR

hello my name is leonor holofernes i'm forty-eight years old and my zodiac sign is taurus with virgo rising tauruses are devoted and patient my favorite book is titled *the marvelous technique* a book about the horoscope and its seven mysteries written by the guru of infinitism allioli rinpoche that i consult every day tauruses are compassionate generous we don't go looking for problems we're peaceful docile obedient

i'm the mother of two daughters amanda and isabel II and i've been married to javier for twenty years in holy matrimony i love my husband i was born to serve him in everything he needs

recently we adopted a lap dog molecule who shits and pisses everywhere if only we hadn't ever gone to that pound one of these days i'm going to give him away without my daughters realizing

we all live together in the valley of the bronx this used to be a NEIGHBORHOOD OF DECENT PEOPLE and now it's become a place filled with druggy delinquents and blacks and arabs and spics let's see if i can make you understand there's   some kinds of immigrants who are nice folk who want to contribute and adapt and go around well dressed and they're like us decent people who learn our language i have nothing against those kinds of immigrants who are educated and work THERE

ARE IMMIGRANTS THAT SEEM LIKE GOOD PEOPLE i'm not racist or anything but

some people who come here are poor and they just come to steal and rape girls i'm talking about those kinds of people who take our jobs when i talk about immigrants who put up mosques all around and practice ablation on their daughters and monopolize the welfare aid that should only be for people from here i have an incorruptible faith in horoscopes my zodiac sign is taurus i've

read in a book that tauruses are compassionate generous we don't go looking for problems we're peaceful docile obedient

i'm peaceful docile obedient

i have faith

faith in the horoscope

faith in eco products

faith in holistic healing and tantra

faith in liposuction

faith in dolce & gabanna gucci lacoste chanel for example there's a store where they sell brands that we used to not be able to get here really high quality expensive brands and meanwhile there are africans out front selling cheap copies of the same brands made in china or who knows where it makes you afraid to go out on the street

just in case i read my horoscope every morning to see what the day holds today it said:

> TODAY YOU WILL FIND EXACTLY WHAT YOU'RE LOOKING FOR . . . BUT IT WON'T BE ENOUGH. IN FACT, NOTHING IS EVER ENOUGH. WHAT'S MORE, THE ALIGNMENT OF THE STARS PREDICTS THAT YOUR SIGN IS GOING TO FACE SOME UNPLEASANT SURPRISES, YOU MUST DEVOTE MANY HOURS TO SOLVING THESE ISSUES. THE FAMILY AND PERSONAL RELATIONSHIPS OF THOSE BORN UNDER THE SIGN OF TAURUS ARE GOING TO SUFFER SOME UPS AND DOWNS THAT MAY EVEN INCLUDE AN UNEXPECTED, UNPLEASANT CONFRONTATION, BUT BY THE WEEKEND EVERYTHING COULD CHANGE BASED ON YOUR PARTNER'S RESOURCEFULNESS, AND YOU WILL HAVE TO DO YOUR PART TO KEEP THE FLAME OF LOVE AND DESIRE BURNING, EVEN WHEN YOUR STRENGTH IS FLAGGING. TAURUS CAN WONDER IF THE STRUGGLE IS

> WORTH IT. THE STRESS COULD BLOW BACK ON YOU THIS WEEK, AND IT COULD END UP GIVING YOU STOMACH PROBLEMS AND LEAD TO TERMINAL CANCER IF YOU DON'T FIND A SOLUTION AS SOON AS POSSIBLE. TIP OF THE DAY: KEEP YOUR YIN CONNECTED TO YOUR YANG AND EVERYTHING WILL BE FINE.

yesterday while my husband walked the dog i went to clean his office and found his computer open and i went into shock there in view were photographs of children in sexual positions or letting adult men fuck them up the butt or practicing fellatio it was all horrible and probably very illegal too

i didn't understand anything my husband is AN EXCELLENT HUS-BAND

i ran back to my room to read the horoscope looking for answers and this is what it said

> BELIEVE IN YOURSELF. EVERYTHING YOU BELIEVE, YOU WILL ACHIEVE. BELIEVING IN YOURSELF IS A REQUIREMENT FOR SUCCESS IN EVERY AREA OF YOUR LIFE. IF YOU BELIEVE THIS YOU WILL ATTRACT THE RIGHT PERSON AND YOU WILL HAVE SUCCESS. IF YOU BELIEVE THAT THIS IDEAL PERSON DOESN'T EXIST, THEN YOU WILL ATTRACT THE WRONG PERSON. IT IS VERY IMPORTANT TO RECOGNIZE YOUR POTENTIAL AND KNOW HOW TO TALK TO YOURSELF. DO YOU HAVE POSITIVE THOUGHTS? OR NEGATIVE ONES? EVERY TIME YOU HAVE NEGATIVE THOUGHTS, THINK ABOUT WHETHER THEY ARE TRUE AND TRY TO THINK POSITIVELY. BE-LIEVE IN YOURSELF AND THAT YOU DESERVE TO BE LOVED AND CARED FOR. YOU DESERVE TO BE LOVED BECAUSE YOU ARE LOVE. YOU ARE . . .

i hear him coming into the house it's late already i stay quiet and i see him enter our older daughter amanda's bedroom i hear him lower his fly i hear my daughter crying but a good wife like me should not interfere with her husband's decisions

i mean that i could think of a thousand ways to murder him whether with poison or a knife but on the other hand i'm sure that the age of aquarius will bring about an age of universal brotherhood linked to reason when it will be possible to solve all the social problems in a fair and equitable way and with more

opportunities for intellectual improvement my husband buys me shoes he buys me jewelry he buys me perfumes when he comes back from amanda's bedroom i don't dare say anything and i pretend i'm watching my favorite soap opera on the tv while

he puts on his pajamas i ask him "do you love me?" that simple question makes

him enraged and he shouts at me   you're a bitch i'll break your fucking shitty face ya fucking nutjob

i'll punch you so many times not even your own fucking mother will recognize you.

you don't have the balls I say you don't have the balls to hit me you are a cowardly bastard all you do is abuse kids fucking faggot son of a mother-fucker now let me watch my soap opera the planet that rules uranus is associated with intuition (the irrational feeling greater than reason)

and the heart's direct perceptions and at a more basic level governs electricity and technology my husband tells me you are a whore he shouts i'll break your fucking face i'll punch you so many times not even your own fucking mother will recognize you

normally it's hard for me to watch tv when the shouting starts but i'm so used to it now oriental astrology associates the current era of

fish with the yin (spirituality and intuition) as for aquarius it represents the yang with an emphasis on rationality and the latest technology our daughters hear us shouting but they haven't complained even once and if they don't complain we can't complain i keep watching our favorite soap opera i think that television shows are important for certain people they help us forget our everyday problems and also tauruses aren't the kind of people who complain really about anyth

J. R.

hey my name's juan ramón calostre but everybody knows me as j. r. i'm thirty and my zodiac sign is sagittarius we sagittarians are idealists but we promise more than we can deliver my favorite color is purple and my favorite book is *the gray notebook or the invasion of the extraterrestrials* by josé llano i think it is one of the great works of neocatalan literature

a lot of people believe in god and i believe in extraterrestrials you got a problem with that? i mean it's a form of faith like any other you can believe in anything liposuction anarchism communism maoism self-help books veganism psychoanalysis feminism television doesn't matter what it is what matters is your degree of implication your degree of faith am i making myself clear i collect everything that has to do with aliens

movies and books about aliens
rocks from other planets
cosmic stimuli
unidentified objects
cylindrical space towers
soundtracks from the universe

secret scientific books

space genealogies

etc.

i believe

i want to believe that there's life out there

during the seventeenth century one of the greatest revolutions in our history took place the closed world of the middle ages opened up to the infinite universe the subject had already been addressed by the greek atomists but they were silenced by other philosophical movements of the time and later by medieval thought giordano bruno during the renaissance was the first who took thinkers like lucretius seriously he said the universe is infinite that

caused a revolution in the era of the inquisition and at the same time a spiritual crisis while medieval man mostly contemplated nature the new modern man aspired to dominate it through technology the world opened up to the infinite universe but in exchange

man lost his place in society and in the world from the philosophical and scientific perspective the concept of the world as a finite and ordered whole disappeared the

previously closed cosmos was replaced by an infinite universe skepticism spread like a fungus as well as free thought with such illustrious names as montaigne bacon and descartes maybe this is the best of all possible worlds but i think there are better ones out there in the universe

i live in a residence hall at the university of saint jeremias it's partly cloudy with a chance of sun and weak winds from the south at dusk there are changes expected for tomorrow but for now there is

total calm today i got a group email through the world contact day site an organization of people who believe in ufos the

email announced an extraordinary gathering on contact with beings from other planets by the IFSB—the International Flying Saucer Bureau—they received a codified message from another world that was sent thousands of years ago two days earlier   the clocks stopped working they stopped working at 15:43 and three seconds exactly i heard on the radio that the cargo ship *odyssey v-37* at the i.s.s.—the international space station—fell into a desert

according to reports from the "space flights center" the ship took off from the i.s.s. at 00:43 GMT and approximately four hours later its charred fragments sank into the waters of the river antuvi 2,500 kilometers east of new barcelona in the valley of the bronx

from my telescope i saw an unidentified visible object it appeared in the night sky before the space station fell   but "nasa" won't confirm or deny i don't want to cause social panic but i watch the sky every day and i know that all that about the clocks stopping and the satellites and space stations falling is no coincidence

this morning i saw an unidentified object floating in the sky i called my girlfriend cristina ladivina i said hey cristina i saw a ufo through my telescope what the actual fuck are you talking about j. r. stop reading so much science fiction she says shut the hell up with it already then i say THIS TIME IT'S REAL i'll pick you up with the car in ten minutes

and don't start doing your makeup or it'll take us thirty thousand years i went and picked up cristina and we drove to the place my gps marked and there was the alien ship calmly levitating amid the trees

here's a photo i took of the spaceship with my phone and i posted it to a website specialized in flying objects

cristina said holyfuck you were right anyhow hurry up i want to get back to the dorm i have to study i have a math exam tomorrow at the university and if i fail i'll kill you

relax, i tell her in the absence of an I the OTHER is just a voice inside us the SUBJECT can no longer be thought of as something foundational but as that which has always been inhabited by the other alterity we are always inhabited by this OTHER who is both friend and enemy

i don't know what the actual fuck you're talking about says cristina and what the hell is that thing floating in the air?

it's just a spinning ovoid object says a voice inside me which i deduce comes from the extraterrestrials and some telepathic technique of theirs the object lands in a clearing and some beings emerge from it then i went over to where the extraterrestrials were i

tried to talk to those beings they were very short and had no asses i tried to speak in advanced level 1 english but there was no need because strangely enough they spoke catalan like a know-it-all philologist   be careful j. r. says cristina don't worry i say to her in the absence of a me

the other is just a voice inside us the subject can no longer be thought of as something foundational but as that which has always been inhabited by the other alterity is that we are always inhabited by this other this other who is both friend and enemy

i don't know what the actual fuck you are talking about says cristina don't rabbit on

then i went over to where the extraterrestrials were

they told me they were the nyargocs an alien race from the planet nyargoc located in the vertex of the vortex of the left side of the fourth solar system they've been visiting us secretly for hundreds of years

i need cash i say to the extraterrestrials i'm broke they cut off my electricity and my phone and i have no job and i'd like to be the first to interview you in an exclusive

the nyargocs told me that one must encourage artistic creation in times of economic crisis and choose a major with a future they taught me to count to ten in their language i thanked them we could learn a lot from these extraterrestrials but they have to fill out the planet earth form i tell them the form includes address phone no. physical and mental maladies id number

but none of the nyargocs have an address who knows what their ailments are they seem like good people i've explained that we humans come from chimpanzees and then i summed up the world for them the ideas of plato and the shift from ancient times to modern the enlightenment and industrialization the atomic age ecology recycling explaining all that to some aliens in ten minutes is no mean feat

the extraterrestrials tell me this isn't their first visit that in fact they've been coming to planet earth secretly since the seventeenth century at least but last week they decided to start a large-scale invasion of the planet

how interesting i say

shut up one of them says we don't give a shit about your opinion what most interests us about you and your human race is your girlfriend say the nyargocs

i see A LASCIVIOUS GAZE in the aliens' eyes and i know what they're talking about

i go over to cristina and i say listen look these guys want to get to know you do me a favor and do what they tell you say yes to anything they ask for

but what the actual fuck are you talking about j. r. have you lost your mind or what she exclaims

it's okay cristina i tell her they just want to get to know you do me a favor and go over there and say hi they just want to talk to you don't be afraid come on go over don't make me look bad we're probably the first human beings to establish contact with aliens don't act the fool remember we can send the exclusive scoop to the local newspaper *the bronx messenger* we'll be famous we'll be in the

history books go on over what's the big deal   fuck off says cristina i don't want to go over there i should be studying for my exam tomorrow you want me to fail or what? fuck your exam you're going over there whether you want to or not i say grabbing her but

she slaps me upside the face and goes back home taking the car leaving me alone with those nyargocs they take off my clothes and start abusing me one after another don't hurt me i beg i came in peace and i have a nervous system and as such the capacity to suffer like any other animal i tell them

exactly you are an animal to us your human brain is a garbage dump compared to ours we can read your thoughts with telepathy 2.0 and since you are a pathetic being you deserve to be treated like an animal get on all fours immediately they order

and i do i get on all fours and i howl and bark i feel ridiculous and stupid while they whip me and stick vibrators into my anus and laugh at me as they make dirty jokes through telepathy i feel denigrated all my humanity has disintegrated i'm nothing more than a larva among giants i start to cry and they

start to devour my extremities one after the other i try to run away but one of them gets mad (!) and shoots his laser pistol (!!) in my face (!!!) and i drag myself away bleeding (!!!!) while i see hundreds of space ships descending from the sky (!!!!!!!) and since they really liked my flesh the nyargocs have decided to CONSUME the entire human race (!!!!!!!!!)

postscript: faith is a question of taste

DOLORS

hello whats up i'm dolors marranxó i'm twenty-seven years old and my favorite color is yellow and my zodiac sign is virgo people born under this sign are kind but shy today i went to the butcher shop downstairs to buy some bacon the pompeu fabra butcher shop since i'm shy an old lady who was in a rush cut in front of

me in line   i decide not to say anything i have no intention of provoking any unnecessary friction i wait my turn patiently reading my favorite book of all time *the lord of the rings of saturn* by j. r. r. tolkien pocket edition they know me by sight for years now at the pompeu fabra butcher shop but i don't even know the names of

the butchers who work there and they don't know mine either i'm no genius of social relations in fact i find humans repugnant which is why even though empirically i know that a better world exists i also know that i will never see it i mean it's not the same thing to live in hobbiton or in mordor just as it's not the same to buy ham in the supermarket or acorn-fed ham from the pompeu fabra butcher shop the pork

was good nice and cheap and besides i liked the butchers dressed in their blood-covered aprons and their brutally powerful hands grabbing enormous knives with the strength of heroes brandishing swords prepared for imminent battle against hordes of sarumans and their uruk-hai flunkies riding their wargs ready and willing to fuck everything up the new epic will be found in butcher shops they are aragorn they are legolas they are gimli they are

what would you like hon? one of the butchers asks me

100 grams of bacon

bacon?

yes 100 grams please thank you

"bacon" is not correct catalan sweetie "bacon" is an anglicism in proper neocatalan we say "cansalada" or maybe "bacó" but never "bacon" says the ultra-serious butcher frenetically chopping the bacon into pieces

excuse me i say i didn't know i've always said "bacon" it's a bad habit like any other

i'm sorry but talking like that is a cryin shame sweetie if we neocatalans stop speaking neocatalan to jabber on in that new spanglish how will our beloved language survive huh?

sorry i didn't want

you didn't want to? or you did want to? mestizos like you who deform the language and turn it into a bastard tongue should be condemned to exile or death

are you nutty as a fruitcake or what? i just wanted to buy 100 grams of bacon i say to the butcher

you illiterate stupidized young people you are the decay of culture the colon cancer of this country if joan orpí the great founder of the neocatalan homeland came back from the dead he would immediately commit suicide just hearing this linguistic bastardization said one of the butchers visibly annoyed

excuse me but this is all getting to be a bit too much i demand some basic manners how can you treat a regular customer like this

the butchers start laughing their teeth are yellow and one of them is even missing an incisor their mouths progressively distort

their amphibian faces darken and dilate

and they sharpen their enormous knives

i try to run away but the door is locked there is no one else in the pompeu fabra butcher shop except me and those three women with bloody aprons and their sharpened knives

i try to open the door banging frenetically but it's locked i scream with all my might but no one responds to my cries for help   and meanwhile the afternoon ripens outside just like every other day

four years studying neocatalan philology at the university of saint jeremias and i have to put up with retards like you said one of them it's a goddamn crying shame isn't it girls? "bacon" says THE HOG-NOSE VIPER HAHAHAHAHA

the three butchers have bloody aprons and all three of them seem very amused and all that but their smiles do not foretell anything good

would j. r. r. tolkien find it as unsettling as i do that so many butchers studied neocatalan philology and were so sensitive about linguistic contamination?

i'm sorry i tell them but i don't think this is any way to treat customers my name is   dolors marranxó and i've been buying meat here for six years and you have no fucken idea of how much i love neocatalan shit i love my language a ton ok? and i don't think there's any need to be

so impertinent who do you think you are to tell me how i should call "bacon" or any other goddamn thing? i go to demonstrations for the neocatalan language i'm a member of obvium cultural and barça and the ateneu and fucking abacus bookstore cooperative i just wanted to buy 100 grams of bacon because i like to eat bacon ok? but now you've made me mad and i'm thinking

of never shopping here ever again and speaking the way i fucken want to   it's too late for that you stupid motherfucker says one of the butchers chopping off my left hand with her sharpened knife as i start to scream in neocatalan while a red almost black liquid comes shooting out of where my left hand used to be like it was a spurting leak on the sink pipe and it stains my clothes my *the lord of the rings of saturn* pocket edition falls to   the floor and its pages get bloodstained and i stain my designer nikes and i stain my whole face and i splatter the white walls of the shop

the last thing my eyes see are the butchers brandishing their sharpened knives pouncing on me and preparing to slice me up

here you have a photo that was posted on the shop's website of me cut into steaks that you can buy on sale for three euros the gram at the pompeu fabra butcher shop bon appetit

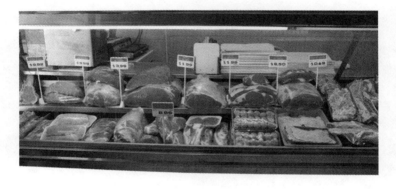

JAUMEJOYCE

hey hey hey hello buey my name is jaume joyce araypuro and I'm a descendiente directo of the line of araypuros who helped that conchudo saint juan urpín to found nueva barselona with mucha blood & violence

I'm thirty-four and a third and I lof roquenrol mi favorite color is verde and mi laburo's thieving it's not easy to be a robber baron in the twenty-first century I make some bizznnes with carpetas and pistolas soy groova chaco so be careful vato hell they won't even know what hit 'em

my vida aquí en el bronx valley is difísil and ya me estoy frizando my culo y cursing the día I left my old sity

so "how did it todo start?"   the otro day mi brother pedrito was murdered by 8 police shots according to la ley 8 legal shots for robbing a '55 chevy ¿and where did they find him? pues in a negro hole all muerto but no one saying nothing at all tremendo

sometimes i remember mi broder pedrito he was a little cocky especialmente when we all wanted to eat olluco con charqui and he insisted on ají de gallina and he didn't like the maicrogüey cause he didn't want to use a fork in the jitachi but he was my brother and I loved him

it was los cops who killed my compa pedrito qué descarados se fue enttyhanded no les gustó la onda qué pigs awebo those killer cops work in the mafia selling confiscated drogas killthepuercos! the police are a scourge all bastards and con la common people son muy verijas the state & federal polise shitty pigs tremendous violacting bro

aquí en the bronx valley nothing matters anymore los kids inhale crack when they grow up they'll make you eat the pavement so be cool don't be culo man chico boludo todos tus chumbos metételo en el culo ¿comprendes mendes?

so in memory of pedrito i'm always rifando in the barrio azul that gang of corrupt puercos pandilleros no tenian chance and we crushed em i broke the jaw of one bato baboso

but they followed me moving uptown with their pickop pero I gave 'em the slip con mi buique and luego i parked the carro dauntaun between a macdónals and a sebenileben where they sell hot-dócs the polise never entran allí afraid to end up on la página dos

since i need dolars pa tener estra incon con efíchensi i went inta a store estaba en la fuácata like a hooker during lent

best stay outta our my way chacos cause the hills have eyes and they're always watchin' cachumambé common common me escapo de los cops and   go inta the store pull out my piece and shout HANDS UP BATOS APÚRENSE

the three empleadas are right then baccuuming they lift up the manos but a salty thick and juicy bosslady dice "Sory míster esquísme plis pero that pistola ➤ is old af papirrín"

hey sista shut the fuck up ok? or I kill ya right now tengo mi funny pinga for your little chicha-chicha he shouts at the beibi comemierda

than she kicks me in the bolas like somesorta chuk norri or the karateka broo li in chinataun and when I turn round another one hits me in the head with something very hebby and i be friquiannndo holly shit

my eyes close

my eyes open

i realise my feet and hands are tied up i'm totally naked

one of the dependientas who goze by the name hauptscharführerin orders me bittte show me yourrr zodiac sign if you don't mind mientras otra me agarra la dicka and sez sheisse está chingón el instrumento and whispers dirty notthings that i can't understand

    buey i say to the piba watch what are yu doing you saramabitch and let me go free or I'm gonna killa ya all i shout you mustabe somesorta machorita gorda y fea put some lotion on those crabs and shave that's what razors are for

    schh! muttis! shut the fuck up machirulo one of them says mocking me wile i estaba en shock what a bomba la morocha! her plunging estaba muy sexy for a vieja con tanto jamón

    she has a PhD in botty shaking she lowers her bragas y descubro su pussy depilado into a swastika   heres a photo they posted on instagram

bitte herr mijo . . . das lasse ich mir nicht gefallen chinwags the one in charge it turns out these bootybuenas speak perfect german because they are servants of satan and también in a nazi cult called "the fiends of hitler" who had once fought on the orders of the third reich next thing i knew the

    nazisexy's forced me to take 5 viagra pills and mi dicka gets hard as a rock not a thing i can do about it and   the aryan pussy fillies rode me and rode me esslow one after the other all night long fuiqui-fuiqui

they had so many curves and i had no brakes i cum ten veces in a row
until my dicka is about to explode damn woman mi bistec está más frío
than a russian toad!

carajo how those guachitas lindas abuse me y relinchan mientras me
linchan and me suckean sacando all my semen dirty bitches . . . ! set me
free puercas! i shout

but they glosan bien golosas in german ein schwul! ein schwul! herr
rat! while they abuse me not a thing i can do high! hell! jaleos!

in the atmosphere floats a stench of semen and shit that mixes with
the steaming aroma of the coffeemachine one by one the fiends violate
me repeatedly while they shout ayyy qué ricooo and chevevere!! another
dependienta put something big in my culo when they bust your culo its
like a mother hugging you with love its like returning in utero

secret garden of delights the last drop on my dicka trembles and falls
and is caut by a slimy forked tongue drop slug! arghg! cascade of laffter
swathed in steams and arrebatado desmadejado they put out cigarette
butts on me neeling las muy vamps

SOCORRO HELP ME i shout but nobody can hear me they already
lowered the shutter ok broder relax your carnitas sie sind des todes! says
one of the fiends as she puts on some reaggeton en un cassette

they shout pompiaera brutal wuuuuuuuuu! ya tú sabes! my feet start
movin as soon as the music starts! guau qué rrrrrico! das ist zum Schreien!
then one of them pulls out a bag filled with excrementos

it was enormous and really heavy and a few days old at least so there
were little worms revolcándose pues toda suavesita y regadita pues they
put it on a paper plate and they put it in my mouth

dieser Dämon ist mächtiger als ihr denkt COME MIERDA PINCHE
BATO CABRÓN MATHAFACKA HURENSOHN

the mierda was all yellow with green stains and blood clots and smelled
like a rotten queso all bitter and salty it was pasty no sabía bien cuando

it stuck in my teeth and on my tongue all viscosa rasposa y pegajosita
the popo was viscosita and when it went down my throat I got sick y me

dieron ganas de vomitar and I puked up what I ate ese morning but I was so hungry that I swallowed los vómitos of caca agria y luego vomité on my trausers de nuevo

come mierda cerdo asqueroso shout las dependientas eat that gooey bubbling salty shit du erbärmlicher Idiot!!!! ayyy qué sabroso y choco-chevere eat that shit that tastes of bile and vomit they shouted while they whipped my face and my erection i was vomiting and i was gargling vomit shit and flegm and wallowing in vómitos

luego las diabólicas de hitler forced me to suck my own verga i bend my rodillas and lift my head my verga is waiting between my legs like a sandwich frito they force me to doblar el estómago some ribs cracked my neck is taut just a few more centimeters i stick out

my tongue and friego la puntita de la dicka its salty y está cubierta de vómito y escrementos mi back se tensa every verterbrae croonches cada rib shreeks with pain i'm a

worm soy un gusano just looking for a bit of love mis bones crack and break but they know how to hide the pain

---

> **HOSPITAL REPORT:**
>
> Male, 38 years of age, named: Jaume Joyce Araypuro.
>
> Approximate date of the accident: Saturday May 30, 05:00 A.M.
>
> Clinical profile: The subject was found on the ground with his spine broken in 4 places and his parietal bone fractured.
>
> Probable cause of the accident: Impossible sexual position.

I ended up en el hospital pero este it's not the end of the historia the moral is don't get mixed up in crime and dont judge those who steal to eat don't forget stay in school and don't rob don't judge the fiends of hitler either pues they were acting in self defensa in the eyes of satan we are all equal

al final we all felt in love y agora we live together yo y estas mamacitas
and we rob bancks pa'vivir como marimberos everybody is japi en nues-
tro matriarcado hitleriano en pas y amor

Ende gut, alles gut!

MOLECULE

hello my name is molecule i'm three years old (which in human terms would be approx 27.14 years) and my zodiac sign is gemini we geminis are nervous and have a great ability to learn quickly my current owners named me molecule because i'm quite

a small dog but everybody calls me "big mo" because they say that that will raise my self-esteem since i'm adopted i have some traumas of a psycho-analytic nature from what i've been able to read on wikipedia dogs are quadrupedal mammals who belong to the canine family in theory i descend directly from the wolf even though i'm not so sure about that i would say that

i have much in common with a wolf i'm short and unkempt when i walk down the street some dogs smell my butt in a friendly way but a lot of other ones simply laugh at me because i'm so short or they completely ignore me just because i'm DIFFERENT

but it's not legitimate to judge someone by their physical appearance or the color of their skin i have all the canine senses highly developed i have great hearing and a fantastic sense of smell capable of defining thousands of different aromas and so i'm equal to other dogs

i know that there are almost eight-hundred different dog breeds but i don't belong to any of them i'm a mixed breed from what i've been told my father was a great dane who mounted my dachshund mother without warning or scruples and then disappeared leaving her alone and knocked up

my mother never loved me it's understandable i was an unwanted puppy a bastard even though dogs are totally social animals my mother never accepted me and she mistreated me cause of her rage and frustration at having a son she didn't want

after a few miserable years which i will spare you here i was adopted by a family the holofernes who named me molecule but the whole family calls me "big mo" to boost

my self-esteem it seemed i'd finally found the love that i had always lacked dogs are animals with a great predisposition to being taken care of by human beings but that doesn't mean that we don't think for ourselves

the holofernes family adopted me to keep their daughters amanda and isabel company they wanted me to be well trained they took me to a school for dogs where they taught me such activities like how to

1. shake hands with humans

2. roll on my back

3. stupidly chase a ball for no reason

4. roll around on the ground feigning joy

5. sit and stand

6. run and do somersaults

7. bark and growl threateningly

grrrr-grrrrrrrrrr and show my eyeteeth etc.

so when i heard MY MASTER'S VOICE i had to do all those silly things without hesitation it was fucking torture and the only thing i learned in that school can be summed up in a single word: OBEY

at home every time any member of the family saw me they would order me to do something: "molecule: find the ball!" "molecule: sit!" "molecule: shake!" it was unbearable i felt like a damn slave

the canine chronicles say that we are totally sociable animals and that we show a predisposition to being taken care of by humans but the truth is that I didn't know any way out of that stupid situation of enslavement until by chance one day while

i was eating breakfast on the news i saw a story about a mutant hamster named manuel who apparently had become internationally famous because he wrote a treatise on animal liberation i ran to the local library and i eagerly read the thesis put forth by that guy manuel about the passivity

of masters his text made my brain explode it was really what i needed to hear and made me reconsider my whole vassalage relationship with the holofernes family they said they loved me but really i was just a servant and they were the masters that's how the world works

but I couldn't stand being on a leash or following that orders from that family of retards then from one day to the next i just stopped obeying and that didn't make the mother holofernes particularly happy and she started to get sick of me she said i stunk and i pissed everywhere and i didn't obey like a normal dog because i wasn't a purebreed when

the others weren't watching she abused me she wouldn't take me out for a walk and i had to urinate on myself she didn't feed me my life became a nightmare because of mrs holofernes one day the old lady put up a sign in the local library as if i were a used chair here is a photo of it that i took on my phone:

Molecule is a handsome and sweet little dog, small and very affectionate, he isn't aggressive, in fact he's very playful, despite having thick white fur he enjoys sunbathing in the afternoon, usually when he's hungry he whines a little to attract attention and get his food he doesn't like to be left alone he loves to go for walks without his leash.

For sale with veterinary chip and leather collar. Interested?
Call 9898779797597998

that stank bitch had put a price on my head before leaving the library i
lifted one leg and pissed right in front of the door while i plotted how to
rebel against that damn old hag

one day the older daughter of the family amanda wanted to play a
joke on her mother who by the way she truly loathed and she wanted me
to play dead she told me "molecule: lay down!" and i had to stretch out
with my belly in the air

and i waited like that for a few minutes like an idiot and visibly uncomfortable until her mother showed up and saw me lying on the floor
and started shouted "molecule is dead! he's dead!" everyone came to see
me the two daughters started laughing less mrs holofernes believed i had
died and i saw her frustrated look when i got up on all four legs moving
my tail happily but she hated me i know it empirically

it was an unbearable situation and i had to end it somehow or other so
one night while everyone was sleeping i went up to the master bedroom
in the second floor hallway i saw mr holofernes going into the bedroom
of one of his daughters to abuse her i took advantage of his absence to go
into the master bedroom

i leapt olympically over the bed where mother Holofernes was sleeping
face up

i climbed on top of her and when she opened her eyes

i jumped on her face and I RIPPED OFF HER NOSE WITH ONE
BITE

while the stupid bitch was still shrieking and bleeding rolling on the
carpet i ran away with the nose in my canines wagging my tail with happiness for the first time i felt like i was descended from wolves

the next day i sent a letter to the newspaper *the bronx messenger* taking
credit for the crime

> *Mrs. Holofernes had to suffer.*
> *There will be more.*
>
> *Signed: "Big Mo"*

and i remembered an article that said that dogs are totally sociable animals and that we show a predisposition to being cared for by humans

so much so that we are known as "man's best friend" but i'm not sure that man is our best friend

and i remembered an article that said that dogs are totally sociable animals and that we show a predisposition to being cared for by humans

so much so that we are known as "man's best friend" but i'm not sure that man is our best friend

and i remembered an article that said that dogs are totally sociable animals and that we show a predisposition to being cared for by humans

so much so that we are known as "man's best friend" but i'm not sure that man is our best friend

and i remembered an article that said that dogs are totally sociable animals and that we show a predisposition to being cared for by humans

so much so that we are known as "man's best friend" but i'm not sure that man is our best friend

MAX

hello my name is max besora i'm forty years old my favorite color is green and my zodiac sign is aquarius those born under that sign are in theory creative people but we don't like it when someone doesn't think like us i wrote a masterpiece titled *the fake muse* and i'm very proud of my work i like its pacing and i like its tone

i know that a title like that can lead to confusion for example the other day i was in a bookstore paging through new arrivals when i ran into an important critic/writer/prize juror/very locally famous commentator

the critic had a monster from the abyss on an iron chain an unnamable beast fearsome and horrific with bloodshot eyes that panted and drooled liters and scratched at the floor of the bookstore with its sharp black claws while articulating the only word that

its master had taught it with a french accent that sounded frankly stupid because it was so contrived: "bodelerrrrrrrrrrrrrrrrrrr arf-arf!" (according to its master the creature from the abyss was referring to the french poet charles baudelaire)

anyway i ran into him in a well-known bookstore and i happened to be carrying a coffee-stained copy of my book in my jacket pocket and i said hello you don't know me but i know you

you are a critic/writer/prize juror/very locally famous commentator and i'd like to show you the book i wrote because i think it's a masterpiece of pacing and tone to see what you think and

i showed him the book published domestically by an anticommercial press here's a photo of the cover posted on the nonprofit publisher's website

the critic/writer/prize juror/very locally famous commentator spent ten seconds reading it with a totally repulsed expression as if he was being eaten alive by some sort of industrial cancer

and it was like funny to see the critic/writer/prize juror/very locally famous commentator standing there trying to hold up the book with one hand and with the other grip the leash of the monster of the infernal abyss who was drooling with rage on the shoes of its master and i couldn't help but let out a little giggle and when he finished looking through the book the first thing he said was

hey but you don't mention any muse you only talk about extreme and senseless violence you talk about really disgusting things stories of perverts rapists sexism and murderers are you

sick in the head or what he says to me besides you don't even know how to write you seem illiterate why don't you write literature that everybody likes about the post-war period or a middle-class family that's what sells you can get famous and win a prize then i had to explain to the critic/writer/prize juror/very locally famous commentator that what i found really disgusting was being a critic/writer/prize juror/very locally famous commentator all at the same time and what's more being a poor empty clone without style very much in line with our diseased and incestuous literary system and at the same time pretending to be a gatekeeper of its essences

then i made it clear that i wasn't a psychopath or a rapist or an abuser but MY CHARACTERS WERE and that only the lame-brained confuse the narrator with the author at this stage of the game

but he didn't understand me and he shook his head to censure me and his monster from the abyss with bloodshot eyes kept saying "bodelerrr-rrrrrrr arf-arf!" with foam between his fangs

the critic added   don't waste your impoverished cultural capital with this sort of book making little stories filled with gratuitous violence your readers might turn violent too what you should do to be a successful author and win awards is

1. make domesticated books that everyone likes

2. go on tv radio and any other media every day and smile a lot

3. have a lot of contacts in the literary world

4. self-promote on social media every day

5. have a famous last name from some wealthy ancestor and milk it

6. be a professional asskisser and make everybody like you

7. all of the above all at the same time

but i thought that literature was the last space of freedom to say whatever we want to i said and not about climbing the career ladder

don't be stupid he says literature is a product like any other and the big publishing houses are the ones that have the money and they need domesticated literature with plots that don't make anyone uncomfortable and language that everyone can understand if you don't do everything i say then YOUR BOOKS DON'T EXIST end of story

it seemed to me that for a critic/writer/prize juror/very locally famous commentator he had no fucking idea about anything i mean he really didn't understand a thing and the critic/writer/prize juror/very locally famous commentator was standing there like a vertical corpse looking at me while his monster from the abyss kept saying: "bodelerrrr" spitting drool on his repulsive claws and

i again tried to explain that *the fake muse* wasn't about gratuitous violence and horror i tried to explain myself by defending my view of literature but we were like two different civilizations speaking mutually incomprehensible languages   and i was so nervous that the words didn't even come out   and i was stammering

> babbling
>
>> gibbering
>>
>>> jabbering
>>>
>>>> nattering

basically i mean that it was frankly useless to add anything more to that conversation and so the only thing that i could come up with in that moment was bitch slapping that famous critic across the face

and he pounced on me in an explosion of uncontrolled fury we both rolled around on the floor

> punching each other

while the monster from the abyss uttered "bodelerrrr . . . arf arf!" and drooled all over my face   and the critic was kicking me and all was blood and pain and all was

grunts/**plaff!**/screams/**arrrrrrggh!**/tears and sobs/**splash!**/falling onto books/**plank!**/biting/**uhhhh!**/breaking shit/**barrabum!**/insults/ **slam!**/strangling/**nyeeeec!**/howls insecurities/**Brrrram!**/snores and sighs/ **blaps!**/scratches/ **rifffs!**/barking/**ffffshh!**/industrial noise/**plonk!**/impropriety/**túúúnnkkk!**/maximum discombobulation/**pam!**/ vast skreich/ **raaaaaaaak!**/gnawing of flesh/**ggggrrrrrrraww!**/ bursts moans/**hich!**/ panting/ **arffff!**/ buzzing/**zzzzzam!**/racket/**clonk!**/thuds/ **patapum!**/ stairs/**cataclong!**/blood/**floshhh!**/earthquakes/**brrrrrum!**/yelps/**grrrrriiii!**/blood loogies

peffff!

JOANA

my name is joana rodríguez but my friends know me as joana carbonara because i'm crazy for spaghetti carbonara i'm twenty-seven years old and i work as a civil servant in the public administration i'm a capricorn caps have a lot of self-control but we don't forgive easily today sandra pérez came over for lunch an inheritrix with strong tight thighs who is also a bureaucrat we met at work

we've been great friends for more than two years or maybe three i can't remember and we have an open relationship within a network of uncommitted relationships she has other close relationships with other people and i do too but sometimes we get together and eat each other out

and after talking about the latest novel by merche rudureda *the attack of the zombies in diamond square* that we'd gifted each other for sant jordi aka international book day we made a tofu salad for lunch while we listened on the ipad to a record by the best band in the world els charango we are both superfans but that isn't particularly original by that i mean

everyone is a charango fan and whoever isn't should be tortured for five years and deserves no respect whatsoever from either of us i mean they could never really be our friend   the music of charango is a tribute to hope for humankind and even though at first glance it seems like a bad ripoff of manu chao it's the best band on the planet every one of their concerts is a ray of light through storm clouds to make this world a prettier and more tender place where we can all be friends and love each other and hug each other in a meadow filled with multi-colored flowers and pink ponies and unicorns where a rainbow is always gleaming like in this photo i took last year on a trip to sweden and posted on my instagram

sandra and i are great friends and we've talked about a ton of things we've always wanted to talk about for example we've joked about running a business together some sort of farm in sisterhood where instead of inseminated and mistreated cows there are men with their penises connected to machines that

every day suck out liters of sperm to fertilize women who of course will live in freedom and dominate the world and that way we'll end the prevailing androcentrism   no more "animal abuse" and more "phallocentric abuse" sandra jokes ha ha

sandra also got me up to date on her lovers she told me now i'm hooking up with a guy who doesn't stop with the mansplaining he complains that i don't shave and he holds the door for me every time we go out and when i warn him about his microsexist behavior he calls me a feminazi he has no idea about anything what a loser

yeah girl i say we have to keep empowering ourselves and fighting against the patriarchy to the max the time of men is ending i'll cut off all their cocks hahaha whoa says sandra that's a bit extreme i mean it's not like i hate men or anything like that a good cock is nothing to sneeze at eh

after lunch we decided to watch a show on netflix one everybody's been talking about with a medieval aesthetic with dragons and lots of sex and violence it was terrible but while we were stretched out on the sofa covered with a blanket i felt warmth between

my legs and i stuck my hand in my pants my cunt was all wet then i smelled my fingers and then i stuck them into sandra's mouth but she told me not today i'm not in the mood

sandra was like super interested in that shitty show for horny teenagers and i on the other hand was superhorny and nervous i hadn't had sex in days and when i don't fuck i get really cranky in general i'm calm i mean you can always wax off

a moustache but you can't always control your moods sandra's moustache and her hairy legs and pits always drive me wild

in the end i couldn't resist

and i pounced on sandra and started kissing her neck but she stopped me saying

but

what

are

you

doing . . . ?

sandra said i already told you i don't want to fuck i have a yeast infection and chlamydia because i've been fucking everything that walks i'm fed up with this polyamory stuff besides i want to focus on my career the only thing i

care about is my job and now i only make friends with people who can offer me professional opportunities and my career is the most important thing

and what about our poly love and our plans to create a matriarchy together i thought you liked me look she says the thing is I'M NOT THAT

INTO YOU that's the truth i mean i like my job more than you and i just want to be friends and to keep up with how your life's going and to weave mutual support webs if you want she says

MUTUAL SUPPORT? i say moving away from her and then we kept watch tv in silence that whole situation was like uncomfortable i was very confused

when we finished watching the show amid a frankly awkward silence sandra told me wait i'll wash the dishes quickly and that way we won't have to worry about washing them later

i told her you don't have to i'll do it later won't take me long

she insisted no i'll do it you made the spaghetti that's not true i said we made the spaghetti together

but i love washing dishes says sandra rolling up her shirt sleeves and turning on the tap really i love it

do me the fucking favor of leaving the goddamn dishes i say pushing her away from the sink it's my house for fuck's sake you're my guest and my friend and i won't let you wash them understood let me SUPPORT YOU

then she i don't know why pushed me into a pile of clean plates that were on top of the marble counter beside the sink and they all fell onto the floor and broke into a thousand pieces stop insisting fuck i'm washing them and that's that says sandra

but what the actual hell i shout i told you not to wash the dishes jesus motherfucking christ i shout jamming a fork in her cheek sandra screams

you are a fucking disgusting piece of shit she says as she grabs a pan and smashes it into my face we are great friends sandra pérez and me she clocks me

with the pan in my face i fall down and she jumps onto me while the charangos are blasting from the ipad and i think about

pink ponies and rainbows i take out sandra's eye with the fork fuck the charangos and the fucking horse they rode in on she gets up and

stomps on my head with her boots i crawl

covered in blood she faints we are great friends

me and sandra and we both work as civil servants in the public administration i cut
    her jugular with the bread knife and liters of blood spurt from her neck
then i
        slowly bleed out i'm twenty-seven years old and a
            capricorn we goat signs are in theory
                                    we're
affectionate and frien

THADEUS

i'm detective inspector thadeus i'm forty-seven years three days one minute and forty seconds old and my zodiac sign is leo we leos are natural-born dominant leaders i've worked for twenty years with the valley of the bronx police if i add up all the

letters of my last name i get the number 7 an important power that has magic virtues i'm obsessed with numbers last month 496 people died in this region and the life expectancy of all those victims can be

expressed by the powers 7 and 9 or the products of those numbers and also with other numbers that have special virtues like the powers of 12 or the perfect number 496 which is equal to the sum of all its factors and which curiously is the exact number of mortal victims last month in the valley of the bronx

blood on the streets of the city of new barcelona

blood on the banks of the antuvi river

blood in the sunsets over abandoned industrial parks

blood on the hands of all the criminals sanctified with the magical liturgy of evil

here in the police station we solve crimes mysteries problems we get cats down from trees we arrest drunks we give traffic fines not to mention dealing with fights between neighbors and such i'm obsessed with numbers for example i proved that there are three hundred souls in this housing development breathing the same carbon monoxide from

five thousand cars that pass by each day heading into the city while the level of violence increases there is like a fever there is a fever in the morning fever in the afternoon fever all night long 104 degrees of fever

i open up the newspaper *the bronx messenger* and read there are five hundred yogurts at half price and tofu went down two percent last month at the supermarket now i only eat tofu every day there are a million

carnivores and i'm eating tofu while in the city there is a mutant hamster destroying buildings shattering glass i calculate

that some two hundred panes of glass are broken at a cost to the public administration of some three thousand euros to repair we should send ten armored police vans and the army to fight that giant hamster ten armored vans shoot ten thousand two hundred rubber bullets the mutant hamster flees and hides in the forest there are between sixty and two-hundred strange murder victims in the valley of the bronx over

the last year plastic bottles that originally held soda actually contained seventeen liters of human fat destined for cosmetic labs the victims were decapitated and

hung from hooks then they placed candles under their bodies to make the fat drip and they also extracted it from the thorax and the cut-up muscles and then they chopped them up and ate their flesh

but if we're talking about violence   a hundred bullets called collateral damage are shot every day in the valley of the bronx and kill a ton of people there are all sorts of gangs there is the pompeu fabra butcher gang who battle the fiends of hitler over territory armed with sharpened knives there are murders everywhere

we have an extremely hairy kidnapper the press calls the king kong of the bronx a psychopath known as the vampire who drinks his victims' blood in movie theaters and as if that weren't enough an alien civilization is threatening to destroy planet earth and every morning i have to read these extremely VOMITIOUS news stories but what can i do in the face of all that? good and evil are subjective products of our minds i mean they're inside and not outside of each of us we are the only ones to blame

evil is the absence of good just like black is the absence of color in fact what i'm saying isn't quite right because something cannot exist without the principle of non-contradiction but i think that what is good for me is not for someone else

the notion of good is multiple but if my notion of good coincides with someone else's then good has to be unique as such i deduce that good is unique and multiple at the same time because deep down

1. existence means suffering

2. the cause of suffering is desire

3. desire is caused by capitalism

4. a way of escaping the suffering caused by desire provoked by capital-
ismis murdering someone and it's my job

to keep that from happening

we've been left without life preservers the width of the vortex compared to the vertex indicates that the levels of violence are surpassing all statistics

the banality of evil is present in every minute in every indifference to injustice plato said that it is not only better to suffer an injustice than to cause it but that it is also preferable to be punished for committing a wrong than to get off scot-free

but to reach that conclusion one has to stop and think in other words put into practice what hanna arendt called critical judgement that ties into kant's idea of thinking for oneself independently and without prejudices and also knowing how to put ourselves in other people's mocassins have empathy any

sane person can commit the most horrible crimes when part of a totalitarian system either out of a desire to ascend ranks within the system or climb the ladder of success by following the rules without reflecting on their actions every day i'm at the station thinking about stuff like this and fighting crime there are profusely unpleasant news stories i stop reading and put *the bronx messenger* down on the desk slowly nothing it says in there can ever touch me because the union of mystical numbers determines how long you'll live and those same numbers make me untouchable

i'm   seven-hundred fifty-three thousand times

untouchable   i'm seven-hundred fifty-three thousand times

untouchable nothing it says   in seven-hundred fifty-three thousand times can affect me i'm

untouchable i'm seven-hundred fifty-three thousand tim

i'm untouchable i'm seven-hundred   fifty-three thousand times untouchab

SMOKE ALMOGÀVERS!
The cigarette for the modern girl!

Why do all the girls seem so modern?
Because they smoke... Almogàvers cigarettes!
Who smokes Almogàvers cigarettes?
Modern girls!

THE BRONX MESSENGER

VAMPIRE RIPS OPEN THE NECK OF A MAN IN A MOVIE THEATER FOR EATING POPCORN TOO LOUDLY!

Ficid quam, simpel ipsam quiaeptatur? Quibustrum ad exerumenihil experorro dit aut dolenih illit, et ommodit aut autemporum ea derrovit aruptistore liqui quaspit et laut eos sequam, everumqui officab orestiae vel ius esentia qui cone voluptios et, iundio. Solore repernatur simus nihic totati volutem et, sim qui sunt et quodiostrum faccat. To dolorioris essus asitatint quid quibus providi tassusapide perum reperro offici atumqui con niet ut acestem resto quae eos mosandi tem doloreperit labor aliquaeptam atiost evellan danisci rectatio. Eri odicillabore nis dolenihil ex estia is dolores tiant. Acia quo qui blabor atia quae nis ma sit aliqua rspeles rem et re, atecusam nesto optatem quamusam

MUTANT HAMSTER

FIGHTS FOR ANIMAL RIGHTS!

Ficid quam, simpel ipsam quiaeptatur? Quibustrum ad exerumenihil experorro dit aut dolenih illit, et ommodit aut autemporum ea derrovit aruptistore liqui quaspit et laut eos sequam, everumqui officab orestiae vel ius esentia qui cone voluptios et, iundio. Solore repernatur simus ndolenihil ex estia is dolores tiant. Acia quo qui blabor atia quae.

MURDERED!

A GANG OF BUTCHERS CHOP UP A CLIENT FOR HIS INCORRECT NEOCATALAN!

MAD SCIENTIST TRANSFORMS INTO A GORILLA AND KIDNAPS SUPERMARKET CASHIER!

Ficid quam, simpel ipsam quiaeptatur? Quibustrum ad exerumenihil experorro dit aut dolenih illit, et ommodit aut autemporum ea derrovit aruptistore liqui quaspit et laut eos sequam, everumqui officab orestiae vel ius esentia qui cone voluptios et, iundio. Solore repernatur simus nihic totati volutem et, sim qui sunt et quodiostrum faccat. To dolorioris essus asitatint quid quibus providi tassusapide perum reperro offici atumqui con niet ut acestem resto quae eos mosandi tem doloreperit labor aliquaeptam atiost evellan danisci rectatio. Eri odicillabore nis dolenihil ex estia is dolores tiant. Acia quo qui blabor atia quae nis ma sit aliquae.

Mandyjane Gets Her Revenge

The curtain rises. Dim lighting. Two men are sitting in a café. The scene plays out naturally, as if they'd rehearsed it many times. Music plays on the radio.

Jaume Joyce Araypuro: Holy shit, mira mi face, man. Do I look happy? Pues no, bato, no estoy nada contento. Am I dead, bato? I feel dead and colonized. Totalmente colonized. I don't feel like belonging here.

Johnny: The night will be dark. There is no moon.

Jaume Joyce Araypuro: El Bronx Valley és una gran boring mierda, brother. ¿Why are we here?

Johnny: Work.

Jaume Joyce Araypuro: Talking to you is like talking to a rock, man. Relaja las carnitas . . .

Johnny: Don't bust my balls.

Jaume Joyce Araypuro: You're wanderful, Johnny. ¿Lo eres o no lo eres? Watchaut my feet, bato, están fuckin' frozen. ¡Cuchi-Cuchi! The streets are all empty aquí. What is esta música de mierda?

Johnny: The ràdio.

Jaume Joyce Araypuro: I wanna kill somebody. Estoy invocando dark forces, vato. I'm loco, guero.

Johnny: That's because you spent too many years in the clink and you've forgotten the world. The bars blocked your view of the outside.

Jaume Joyce Araypuro: Todo es pura darkness . . . Dreaming es difícil, brother. Mira mis fingers are trembling. I wanna kill gatos just fo' fun.

Johnny: Don't start getting paranoid. That's like when you stare into a washing machine on the spin cycle. Everything is going round and round until you feel nauseous, you get me?

Jaume Joyce Araypuro: No, I don't understand you, Johnny. No entiendo tus palabras. I don't wanna understand nada.

Johnny: There's nothing to understand. We're here for work. Thank God you have a job. If we behave, we won't have to go back behind bars. We'll be free. That's what they call parole.

Jaume Joyce Araypuro: To hell con parole! Estuve en el jail after I was raped and forced to eat my own mierda and mi dicka by a sect of Nazi women . . . The Fiends of Hitler, ever heard of 'em? . . . I fought back, ¿comprendes mendes? . . . I had to . . . I had to kick, I had to fight with . . . four or five batas . . . ¡ARF-arf-grrr-arf! . . . los dientes fuera . . . I had to fight back and I hit them, sabes, I hit them and I hit them and . . . I kicked them and . . .

Johnny: They forced you to eat your own shit? Hahah . . .

Jaume Joyce Araypuro: No, I fought back, muy duro y . . . yo me resistí . . . tuve que . . . tuve que dar patadas, kick 'em in da face . . . tuve que pelearme con . . . cuatro o cinco boogie women delante mío . . . I was too . . . too focused on el fighting to notice their physical . . . eh . . . física, porque ellas . . .

Johnny: Yes?

Jaume Joyce Araypuro: They . . . were attacking me.

Johnny: What were they doing to you?

Jaume Joyce Araypuro: Oh, ellas estaban . . . estaban en . . . estaban . . . they surrounded me, y todo lo demás . . . y me estaban atacando y me tuve que defender, fight, fight, and defend myself y coger palos . . . aunque luego viví con ellas not so long time ago.

Johnny: ¿«Coger palos»?

Jaume Joyce Araypuro: Yes, coger palos, gather up sticks.

Johnny: When I was little I played a game of gathering up sticks and throwing them as far as I could.

Jaume Joyce Araypuro: ¡Yo también, brother! ¿You played that too?

Johnny: Yes!

Jaume Joyce Araypuro: ¡It's fun! ¡JA JA JA!

Johnny: You want to go back to the clink? Because I sure as hell don't.

Jaume Joyce Araypuro: I'll die fighting before I go back to la trena, man, I swear to you on San Juan Urpín.

Suddenly, a sound. The two men turn to look. KingKong stumbled over something as he was leaving the bathroom.

KingKong: Uh-uh! Shit . . . this bar is really dark. And outside is too. Everything is darkness. Even I am dark and ultrahairy. So what? This café is like a box of dead people. They told us that today the machine would come and we're still waiting. Shitty job, shitty life . . . I'll destroy the fucking radio. I'll break this plastic table. I'll destroy that bathroom for midgets that's always clogged with shit. I'll destroy the fucking gas stove and the disgusting microwave. And then I'll grab a can of gas and set fire to the fucking place. Uh-uh!
Johnny: Calm down, don't go apeshit.
Jaume Joyce Araypuro: Yeah, cálmate bato, no seas pinche asshole.
Johnny: The machine's just arrived.

The three men look at the machine, curious.

KingKong: What kind of a machine is that?

Johnny: It's an Intelligent Machine the parole officers sent us so we can do our job. I don't know how it works.

Jaume Joyce Araypuro: There must be un botón . . . un bo-tón rojo . . . watchaut, aquí, ¿you see it, brother?

Johnny: Yeah, yeah, we just have to press the button and pressurize everything.

KingKong: This is some bullshit. I don't like this machine at all. I hate these enslaving machines. I'm an anarcoprimitivist and I demand a return to the preindustrial era.

Jaume Joyce Araypuro: Ugly machines, man . . .

Johnny: Shut up. Quit complaining. We're here to work. I couldn't care less whether you like the machine or not.

KingKong: Everything is upside down. Everyone has really horrible hairdos and everybody ends up in prison or shot or their kids get sick and there's something I can't put my finger on fucking everything up, in a million surprising ways. Uh-uh!

Johnny: Now that the machine is here, we've got work to do. We have to go to the house of (*he looks at some papers and a map*) . . . the Holofernes family.

Jaume Joyce Araypuro: That's in the burbs, man.

Johnny: Exactly. I want you both ready to go in five minutes. Finish your cigarettes and let's go.

Jaume Joyce Araypuro: We don't pay attention to the keys until we come up against a locked door. Cray-cray, bato . . . !

A large house rises, imperial, amid a hectare of civilized lawn. It is the home of the Holofernes family, an almost perfect reproduction of the Versailles Palace. The eldest Holofernes daughter, Amanda Jane, is in her room singing a song. Her younger sister, Isabel II, plays with a phone next to her.

Amanda: Oh, Isabel II, I hate this house and its rococo decoration, I hate Dad and Mom, they give me nightmares. I hate every little thing about this place and I hate this place. The only thing I respect is my dog, Molecule, because he ripped off my mother's nose hahaha.

Isabel II: I'm chadding wit my noo smartphone.

Amanda: Listen to me, Isabel II. Put down your phone and listen to me when I talk to you. My life is horrible and yours will be too when you learn to think for yourself and not through a machine. But look: I'm not just talking about me, but about the whole family. I hate you all. I find you truly detestable and I'd like to see you all die in a thousand horrible ways. I hate our father and the way he smells of rancid cock. I wish he were dead. I hate Mom and all her true lies and false truths. I wish she were dead. And I hate you too, my little sister, because you're perfect. And in your perfection I see my misfortune reflected.

Isabel II: I dive deep inta the virtual worl. Bois rite me nazty stuff and sen me fotos of there diks.

Amanda: Listen to me, little sister. Pay attention, I'm begging you. Really, it's deeper than all that, much deeper . . . because all this hatred I feel toward you, my own family, affects me physically, affects my brain cells. I haven't gotten my period in weeks. I have stupid allergies. I associate the word "dad" with diarrhea.

Isabel II: Whatevs. I lurve dating apps. They lite up my imaginashun. Fiddy-year-old perverds send me fotos. Look, Mandy, look how the gizz cums outta this ole guy's wang with liddle drops of blood.

Amanda: My skin is gross. I spent all day smearing my face with an incredibly expensive and repulsive cream. I don't have friends anymore. I have panic attacks. And psoriasis. Or maybe it's leprosy, what do I know. My skin gets red and then falls off in chunks. In fact, it's affecting my ability to breathe. One of these days I'll suffocate, fall down dead at lunchtime, ploff, my head in a plate of spaghetti. Oh, wouldn't that be charming!

Isabel II: I type fast. Im anonymouse in the virtual whirl. Then I sing a song. Then I send emojis to my virtual luvers when they sen me fotos of theyre dicks.

Amanda: No. I'm not the one who has to die. It's our parents who have to die. It's for you, Isabel II, you're the reason I haven't set fire to this house with everyone inside.

A middle-aged woman suddenly opens the door. Amanda Jane stops speaking. Mrs. Holofernes walks into the center of the room. Her only indisputable feature is her mouth hanging open after hearing what her daughter just said. That, and that she has no nose. The family dog, Molecule, ripped it off a week earlier.

Mrs. Holofernes: (*with a nasal voice, ironically*) I heard you, Amanda. I know what you think. Daughters shouldn't think those things about their parents. You are such a Scorpio. According to this week's horoscope, Scorpios are going into a lunatic phase with little chance of any professional success. By the way, I made an appointment at the vet. Next week I'm having Molecule put down. After he ripped off my nose my life has been hell. He's a demented dog and he needs to be put to sleep.

Amanda: I won't let you put Molecule down! I'll kill you first, you witch!

Mrs. Holofernes: How can you say such things to your mother!

Amanda: Fine, Mom. Fine, let's speak our minds. You want me to speak my mind? Fine. I hate you and Dad because you're both depraved perverted abusers. OK? I hate your rancid smell and I wish you were dead.

Mrs. Holofernes: That's a horrible thing to say, Amanda. Unpleasant. Vile. Sinful. I will not tolerate you speaking like that about me!

Amanda: You are dead inside and out, Mom. And not only do I want you both dead but dead and gone. Chopped up. Quartered. And my name is Mandyjane, not Amanda!

Mrs. Holofernes: For God's sake . . . you're crazy!

Amanda: God? You are bringing Him into this, Mom? You who fuck men you don't even know, truck drivers, married men, johns, doctors, postmen, milkmen, moving men, teachers, nurses, trapeze artists, bricklayers, poets, shopkeepers, politicians, detectives, Portuguese senators.

You fuck everything except your husband the pederast! No, Mother, don't mention God with impunity.

Mrs. Holofernes: What you are saying is not nice, not nice at all.

Amanda: . . . And we both know why you won't touch him. I remember my childhood, when he would come into my room at night, how he caressed me . . . And you, Mom, you who bring up God, you didn't do anything to stop him. You are just as evil and depraved as he is for hiding it and sticking your head in the sand.

Mrs. Holofernes walks over to Amanda and slaps her hard. They both cry, while the younger sister, Isabel II, keeps playing with her top-of-the-line smartphone.

Amanda: I'm sorry, Mom. I didn't want to . . .

Mrs. Holofernes: I know, I know you didn't want to.

Amanda: I didn't want to . . .

Mrs. Holofernes: You didn't want to. You didn't dare. You weren't thinking.

Amanda: I didn't want to. I didn't dare. I wasn't thinking.

Mrs. Holofernes: I know, Amanda, you didn't want to, you didn't dare, you weren't thinking. That's that. Let's put it behind us. Everyone says and thinks horrible things sometimes. People do strange things when they get bored. Wars, murders, art, that's how we find comfort when we're bored. You have to do something. Go to the University of Saint Jeremies. Read your horoscope. Sign up for ice hockey. Build a birdcage. Do something good, Amanda, otherwise you'll end up like those three ex-cons who are fixing the stable, lost, wretched, done for.

Amanda: Yes Mama. Whatever you say, dearest Mother (*inside, Amanda is thinking: fucking shitty witch, first chance I get I'll flay you like a sow, I'll slice up your tits, I'll cut off your head and impale it from the highest belltower*). Farewell, sweet mother of mine!

The three ex-cons arrived early that morning to the Holofernes estate. They've been working for three hours, fixing the stable with a strange machine.

Jaume Joyce Araypuro: La neta esta vaina es bien culera, brother. I wasn't born for this work shit. No vine al mundo con este purpose, man. I know for shure que fate had sumpin better planned for me. For example . . . not working.

KingKong: Quit complaining. You're always complaining. We've only been here for an hour and you're already complaining. Does that seem normal to you? Does it? Uh-uh!

Jaume Joyce Araypuro: Damn it, man! I could be un actor en Holibud y ganar millones, bato . . . !

KingKong: These people must be disgustingly rich. Did you notice that car? A '77 Mustang. Wow.

Jaume Joyce Araypuro: Yeah, está bien chido el carrito.

KingKong: They have a Mercedes, too. And a Chevrolet. And a SAAB.

Jaume Joyce Araypuro: SAABs are Jewish cars.

Johnny: That's not true. Don't make shit up.

Jaume Joyce Araypuro: I'm not making up nada, buey. You're the liar. You told me you've only ever killed one person pero estoy convencido que eres un mass murderer, man, un psycho . . . !

Johnny: I'm not gonna argue with you. I need to piss like a racehorse.

KingKong: I've always wanted to see other worlds but I'm never allowed in. They always say I'm not wearing the right jacket. But I know that it's because I used to be too bald, and now I'm too hairy. I'd also like to be more free, until I realize that I'm too locked up inside myself. I'd like to have a family like the Holoferneses and live with Queen Kong in the jungle. Uh-uh!

Johnny: I really gotta piss. I'll be back.

Johnny walks toward the Holofernes home. In the entryway he runs into young Amanda, who just happens to be passing by.

Johnny: Hello.

Amanda: Who are you? You don't look like you're part of my family. I've certainly never seen you before. Are you some brother they never

THE FAKE MUSE - 105

told me about, who ran away from home at four years old to traffick diamonds in Africa or something like that? Are you the mailman? Some finance genius? Are you a homeless bum here to rob us? We have a lot of valuable things here. You could take all my mother's jewelry. It's in the safe in the second bedroom on the second floor. The secret code is 679568878323677.

Johnny: I'm not your secret brother, the mailman, or a burglar. I'm not looking for jewels, just a pot to piss in. Who the hell are you?

Amanda: I'm like an Amazon, but I'll never cut off a breast to shoot arrows easier. I'm too fond of my rack.

Johnny: I must say you do have an incredible body.

Amanda: Thank you. The secret to my smooth glowing skin is simple: all I have to do is sleep in a king size refrigerator three times a week. I'm Mandyjane, by the way. What's your name?

Johnny: My name is Juan Pons, but everybody calls me «Johnny Dynamite».

Amanda: Not the greatest nickname but you look kinda dangerous with all those tattoos. Are you going to rape me?

Johnny: No, I'm not going to rape you. I'm working . . . I'm putting up beams, roofing.

Amanda: Very interesting. A truly interesting job.

Johnny: Thank you.

Amanda: Fascinating.

Johnny: Thanks.

Amanda: Amazing.

Johnny: Thanks.

Amanda: Astounding.

Johnny: Thanks.

Amanda: Mind-blowing.

Johnny: Thanks.

Amanda: Would you like a tonic water? On the house.

Johnny: Sure. But first I need to use the toilet.

Amanda Jane points to the bathroom. Afterward, they each sit on stools in the kitchen. She notices Johnny's boots: they're covered in mud.

Johnny: This house is enormous.

Amanda: It's an imitation of the Palace of Versailles. 🏰 A repetition. A simulation. Constructing the adequate decodifying mechanism to apply to the inner message. Versailles is not Versailles.

Johnny: Yeah.

Amanda: I like your dirty old boots. I'm fascinated by everything old and dirty. I'm fascinated by the most horrible, forbidden things. I'm fascinated by filth and perversity. Sometimes I wish I were a character in a soap opera, you know the kind: poor-girl-marries-rich-old-man-he-mistreats-her-and-she-takes-her-revenge.

Johnny: Aha.

Amanda: I'm fascinated by ugliness, annoying pranks, I'm fascinated by everything unexpected and sordid.

Johnny: Aha.

Amanda: I'm fascinated by disfigurement, the mental and physically handicapped and all the jokes about them, I'm fascinated by serial killers and the great horrors of humanity, I'm fascinated by repulsive and violent people.

Johnny: Aha.

Amanda: Is "aha" all you know how to say or what?

Johnny: Maybe I don't have anything to add.

Amanda: Maybe you're just an idiot.

Johnny: Maybe so.

Amanda: Maybe I should tell my father that you tried to molest me and that will get you fired and, with any luck, back in prison.

Johnny: You won't do that.

Amanda: Oh, no? And why wouldn't I, tell me, why not?

Johnny: No one would believe you.

Amanda: You're wrong. You're completely and utterly wrong. Everyone thinks I'm an adorable young thing. Pretty and adorable. I have a reputation as an adorable girl. A solid reputation. Why wouldn't they believe adorable Amanda Jane over some random stranger from god knows where, covered in tattoos, who looks like he just got out of prison?

Johnny: I did just get out of prison.

Amanda: Ohmigod! Were you really in prison?

Johnny: Really.

Amanda: And that's why you have all those tattoos?

Johnny: Yeah.

Amanda: This tattoo is of a woman. Who is she? Is she your wife? Your mother? An aunt?

Johnny: She's an ex of mine, from Mexico.

Amanda: Whoa. And . . . and what's it like behind bars? I mean it must be savage in there, right? Filled with guys fighting all the time, filled with testosterone, violence and semen in the showers, right? And why'd they put you in the clink? Did you mug a defenseless old lady? Rob a bank? Stick up a gas station?

Johnny: That's none of your business.

Amanda: If you don't tell me, I'll tell Papà that you tried to rob the house.

Johnny Don't be ridiculous.

Amanda: I'll scream really loud. I'll scream so loud that in less than two minutes you'll have ten cops pointing their guns at you.

Johnny: You wouldn't do that.

Amanda: Oh yes I would. I'm suuuper crazy. I definitely would do that. Do you want to try me?

Amanda Jane screams, but Johnny quickly covers her mouth.

Johnny: You are crazy.

Amanda: You see? I warned you. I'm *almost* eighteen. I'm not a kid. Didn't you notice my tits? They're perky and supple (*she fondles her breasts*), I'm young and I want to know what got you put behind bars.

Johnny: I killed a man in a movie theater because he was making too much noise eating popcorn and I couldn't concentrate on the movie (excuse me, *film*). I bit him.

Amanda: Fuck, holy shit . . . that's amazing! You're a vampire! Johnny «the Vampire»! It's an incredible feeling to be with a real authentic murderer! It's like incredible. It's like . . . arousing. In fact, my panties are dripping.

Amanda runs her hands over her breasts and her crotch. Johnny combs his black hair back with a comb he's pulled out of his pocket, while he checks out the girl's ass. He can almost see her butt cheeks because her skirt is so short. Johnny draws close to the girl and embraces her from behind. Amanda turns and . . .

Amanda: . . . our mouths fuse together, lustfully. His hand makes its way down to between my legs, over my damp panties. I stroke his hard cock through his pants. If only he'd shaved; his facial hair is so rough and irritates my skin, as if he had a crown of thorns on his face (now that I think about it, I haven't waxed in a week: I must seem like a yeti, but I give zero fucks). While our tongues intertwine, he runs his hands over my boobs. He pulls down my dress (I never wear a bra) and licks my hard nipples. Then he puts his hand between my thighs. I'm sopping wet. Johnny kneels down in front of me and lifts my skirt and lowers my g-string. He stares at my dark, thick lips, brings his mouth close and takes a big whiff of my cunt. First he aggressively licks my clitoris from top to bottom. I'm dripping. Then he tongues my anus for a while before returning to my cunt, timidly biting my vaginal lips, which contract slightly from the pain and pleasure. "Hit me down there," I order. Surprised, he punches me on the pussy, not too hard. I'm so excited. Why do we ponder the eternity of the universe when what we really want is a S&M porn manual? He keeps sucking my lips, swollen with pain and pleasure. Before I come I pull his head from between my legs, while I fondle his crotch and stick my tongue in his mouth. His lips are covered in my juices. Kissing him is like licking my own pussy. I appraise the size of his member and delicately unzip his pants. The sound of the zipper is drowned out by Molecule's barking in the backyard. I get down on my knees and open his pants. I observe his penis, hard and red, and first I start to masturbate him, slowly, without making any sudden movements. Then I place his gland into my mouth, noting ▬▬▶ how it grows bigger, licking his balls and sucking on his erection with a ton of saliva while I jerk him off. He can't take it anymore and he grabs me, placing me on top of the table with a pleasant violence. I open my legs and see his penis seeking refuge in my throbbing cave. He enters me so deeply and delicately and brutally, all at the same time, and I am panting while he moves his pelvis. "You like that?" he asks me, politely. Fuck polite. "Don't talk, just fuck me," I say. And in and out, in and out, that's the history of civilization. Men searching in my hole for what they will never find in themselves. Horny, I grab his ass and squeeze him to me, while he rhythmically pumps. His eyes shine powerfully. There is no face more beautiful than his as he fucks me. Johnny is virile and stupid and masculine, but his primitive idiocy excites me. I push him off me and turn around, my back to him. I order him to fuck me up the ass. First he licks my asshole again, so it's well lubricated, and then he places his cock at the wrinkled entrance. He presses slightly, making me moan softly. A second attempt makes the hole dilate a little more. On the third attempt I feel the immense pressure of his cock entering my ass. His seventeen centimeters drilling my anus are like an ocean wave swallowing you up and, as he fucks me from behind, I masturbate roughly until I explode in an intense orgasm and a small spurt even comes shooting out of my vagina as if my water had broken. But I still want more. His tattooed, scar-covered body makes me horny, and now I stroke his sweat-soaked body and I move down again to his crotch, licking his trembling gland, half-deflated from the effort. He lies back on the floor and opens his legs, and I stick my tongue in his ass. As he pants with pleasure, I notice his erection has returned. I suck energetically on his cock for a while and, when it's good and hard, I order him to penetrate my cunt. Like a slave, submissive, he obeys and thrusts, sweating like an animal in danger of extinction, pounding against me harder and faster . . . the frenetic rhythm increases . . . as does the moaning . . . our mouths draw closer . . . I bite his lips and they bleed a little . . . each time he penetrates me more fiercely and brutally, as if trying to break my pussy, until I almost cum for a second time. But no, sometimes I think I'm about to and it's just a false alarm. Johnny still hasn't bust a nut so, with my vagina still dripping, I get down on my knees again and put his throbbing cock into my mouth, sucking on it viciously. It tastes of pussy and shit. He fucks my mouth until he starts to tremble, saliva mixed with his discharge falls from my lips, as he goes in and out faster and faster until he tells me he's about to blow his wad. That turns me on and I masturbate again with one hand while I feel his cock like a volcano about to erupt. "Thar she blows . . ." he says in a wisp of a voice. And just when all the semen shoots into my mouth (salty, my fertilized taste buds inform me) I climax too amid moans of pain as if all the evil inside me was escaping through my vagina and I tell him "I love you" ♥ with his cock still in my mouth. After I swallow, I lie on the floor completely spent while Johnny shakes his cock, releasing the remaining sperm from his balls. The white liquid falls slowly to the floor like drool just as my dog, Molecule, comes in through the door and starts licking up the semen, thinking it was eggnog or condensed milk. "Get out of here," I shout at the dog throwing a slipper at him while I think that no one ever asked me if I wanted to be born. I'm a woman, can't you see what I am, what they've made me into? Because all this is about suffering

    about lips smeared the color of "passion fruit"

    about writing bastardly on purpose

    about doing everything in the most criminal way possible

    about lubricated and quartered cocks

    about bad erotic literature

about music playing on a distant radio
about loving someone who doesn't want to be loved
about gardens with no flowers
about feeling sympathy for the devil
about cosmic stimuli
about dancing the mambo barefoot over hundreds of putrid corpses

The lights go out and, after a little while, come back on. Amanda Jane and Johnny are stretched out in a bed.

Amanda: You're the love of my life, Johnny.

Johnny: You can't say that, we only met ten minutes ago.

Amanda: OK. Did you like the blowjob? And the anal sex? I love you.

Johnny: «I love you» is too much, too powerful of a statement. It demands special treatment, you can't just go around saying that casually.

Amanda: Whatever. Doesn't matter. We just met and five minutes later we were fucking. I told you I love you while I was sucking your cock too and you didn't complain then.

Johnny: It's not the same thing. I was focusing on shooting a load into your mouth. It's true you had my penis in your mouth and at the same time you said you loved me (and the scene was pretty comic, I'll admit), but I don't think that was the best moment for a declaration of love, I think a good moment would be while strolling by a river, or leaving a movie with subtitles, or sitting on a wooden bank on a deserted avenue in mid-October, but no, you had my penis in your mouth and at the same time you said you loved me, okay, fine, but I don't think that was the best moment for a declaration of love, I think that a good moment is when you've known each other for (at least) a week, or when you know each other's last names, or when you know each other's birthdays, but no, you had my penis in your mouth and at the same time you said you loved me, but I don't think that was the best moment for a declaration of love, I think a good moment would be when you don't have someone's penis in your mouth and my fist simultaneously penetrating your anus, or when someone isn't burning your nipples with a lighter while you feel something terribly painful ripping your body and another cock in your mouth all at the same time, but no, you had my penis in your mouth and at the same time you said you loved me but, frankly, I don't think that was the best moment for a declaration of love.

Amanda: If that was an attempt at a poem, it's a very bad poem. In any case, I do think it was a good moment. It's always a good moment for everything: fucking, loving, getting to know each other. It's all just words, Johnny dear. Rape, pederasty, trauma. It all comes from the same virginal ray of light.

Johnny: I don't know what the hell you're talking about.

Amanda: My father . . . is the Expulsion of the Triumphant Beast . . . it's a terrible story. And my mama, well, that's another terrible story. And my little sister is another . . .

Johnny: Terrible story.

Amanda: Exactly. I hate my parents. I hate them, I hate them, I hate them. Don't you want to know why? I'm wounded, dear Johnny. I'm ugly. I'm a ghost, the shadow of a shadow. This is going to be my year, the Year of the Ghost. I need you, Johnny dear.

Johnny: If they catch me in your bed they'll fire me. I can't lose my job. If I lose my job I go back to the clink.

Amanda: I feel guilty, I feel trapped. I feel imprisoned in my own past. I need you.

Johnny: I don't want to get fired. I don't want to break parole.

Amanda: I'm fat, I used to be too skinny, now I'm too wounded. And too ugly. I need you, Johnny dear.

Johnny: And now you're furious with your parents.

Amanda: Now I'm furious with my parents. I hate my father. He's a rapist, a perverted repugnant pederast. It's his fault, and Mama's for allowing it, that my life is hell.

Johnny: I understand.

Amanda: What do they do to pederasts in prison? Do they beat them? Do they mutilate them? I would cut their cocks into slices. Do they cut their cocks into slices?

Johnny: They punish them.

Amanda: Well we have to punish my parents. We have to kill my parents.

Johnny: No. Impossible. It's illegal, anti-constitutional. What you should do is turn them in and have a judge decide their fate.

Amanda: The justice system is a joke. It's better to take the law into your own hands. I want to see them die. It must be a beautiful sight. We'll do it together.

Johnny: It's not a beautiful sight. It's not a spectacle, it's not film, it's not TV, it's not theater, it's not fiction.

Amanda: Why not?

Johnny: Well, because when you kill someone it isn't beautiful or ugly. It's . . . prohibitive. Otherworldly. Anti-natural. It's a crime, original sin.

Amanda: I like being anti-natural. I don't believe anymore in miracles or the social contract. I don't believe in anything anymore. The law has always been dictated by men, and in my particular case by my father, and I can't stand it anymore.

Johnny: I don't understand a word you're saying. You're too young for me.

Amanda: Actually I'm too old for anyone. I love you, Johnny. Let's go far away from here, where nobody knows us, where nobody will ever know us, where we just have each other with no need for anybody else.

Johnny: We'll sleep in cheap motels with neon signs.

Amanda: We'll make love in gas station toilets.

Johnny: We'll buy an old farm and plant tomatoes.

Amanda: I'll take care of you and you'll take care of me. What do you say? If we sell Mama's jewelry and dresses and my father's cars, we can live like kings for twenty years minimum and maximum. We can set up a business. A hotel, we can open a hotel in New Barcelona, a cute little hotel near the sea where we can grow old.

Johnny: Sounds good. Sounds different. Sounds fantastic. Sounds impossible.

Amanda: It sounds like happiness, Johnny. Sounds neat and tidy. Sounds empirical. There's just one easy thing that has to be done so we can be that happy.

Johnny: Kill your parents.

Amanda: Exactly. I've planned it out to the last detail. We have to do it tomorrow. I will spend the day on the riverbank, picnicking with my parents. You'll come later. You'll bring a gun, the gun my father keeps in his desk. You'll point the gun at his head. The gun will go bang bang. We'll make holes in papa's head. Then I'll fill his balls with lead. Oh . . . it'll be so fun!

Johnny: Burglary is a crime: we could get three to five years. If you rob a bank, five to ten years. If you kill someone, you won't get out of prison.

Amanda: Except if you kill your own family. I read it in a teen magazine a few years ago. I don't remember what it was called but it had horrible electric-colored covers. Tomorrow. You and me. We have to do it tomorrow. Tomorrow. Tomorrow.

Johnny: Tomorrow.

Amanda: The sun'll come out . . .

Johnny: Shit. OK. Tomorrow.

Jaume Joyce Araypuro, who had gone to the toilet, heard the entire conversation. He runs off. Police station. They knock on the door of Detective Inspector Thadeus's office. A policeman enters.

Policeman: Sir, there's a guy here, Jaume Joyce Araypuro, a mestizo from New Barcelona, who wants to talk to you. Talking 'bout some story of rapes, murders, and teenage criminals. It seems as important as it is repulsive.

Detective Inspector Thadeus: Criminals? They're everywhere. At the night bus stops, in lonely lots, behind meager stubble fields. They are here and there, today and yesterday, in the future and in prehistory. Murderers and rapists! They hide in the frozen food section of empty clandestine supermarkets. What do they want? To rape you! They fall out of windows, sometimes, with drool hanging from their lips. What are they looking for? Holes! Their eyes are filled with lust. You see them? It's them! You recognize them?

Policeman: He says it's urgent, sir. I think that Evil is about to be unleashed.

Detective Inspector Thadeus: Evil? What exactly do you think Evil is? In Romance languages like Latin, there is no distinction between "bad" and "evil." In other languages, for example English, there is *good* and *evil*. *Evil* is morally bad, while bad in the sense of harm, prejudice, disgrace, affliction, calamity is just bad. Just like in German with *Gut* and *Böse*. *Böse* is the same as *evil*, while *Übel* is bad in the sense of "harm, prejudice, disgrace, affliction, calamity," like in English. Leibniz distinguishes between the «malum metaphysicum», bad derived from a defect of creation, and the «mal morale», *evil* in English or Böse in German . . .

Policeman: Puah. What are you trying to tell me, sir?

Detective Inspector Thadeus: What I want to tell you, oh policeman in service to the community, is that evil is very easy to identify. Evil is what injures us, causes us pain, and, in the worst cases, can end up killing us. Human beings are endowed with sensors that prevent and warn against evil. But there is a congenital illness in some individuals, an insensitivity to pain, that leads to evil. So we could say that this mechanism of evil or pain works in our favor. Good, on the other hand, is tricky and slippery, since it is always a transitory situation between painful situations until finally we die.

Policeman: That's all very well and good, sir, very deep, I like your tone and style, sir, but . . . I don't understand a word. I was trained by the academy to fulfil law and order—if necessary with unnecessary violence—and I'm no friend to abstract thought. What I'd like to know is what do we do with the mestizo waiting outside for the last hour?

Detective Inspector Thadeus: Send him in.
Policeman: Yes, sir.

The policeman exits and enters again accompanied by Jaume Joyce Araypuro, who sits down in a chair in front of the inspector's desk.

Detective Inspector Thadeus: Who are you? What is your name? Are you a communist? What is your value scale? You're a foreigner, that I can see, but what's your story? We all have a horrible story to tell.
Jaume Joyce Araypuro: My name doesn't matter, buey. What matter now is what's about to go down, ¿comprendes mendes? And what's about to go down is pretty much important como para que me listen, bro. Eso sí, you have to promise me que no vuelvo al jailhouse, man.
Detective Inspector Thadeus: You're asking for a lot. First tell me the story, and then maybe we can negotiate.

Jaume Joyce Araypuro explains the whole affair while Inspector Thadeus listens and smokes, Almogàvers™ cigarettes.

Detective Inspector Thadeus: The Holofernes family. Ex-cons. A resentful girl abused by her father falls in love with a tattooed man and they plan a murder. Very well. Is that all?
Jaume Joyce Araypuro: Es todo, man. In exchange quiero protecsión oficial and una casa en las Bahamas. Deal?
Detective Inspector Thadeus: Deal, Judas. You don't mind if I call you «Judas», do you? We have to put an end to crime. Danger on the streets. Danger for the population. People are so scared they don't even dare go out on the street. The insanity of violence. Grandmas left without grandchildren. The murderers hide like rats, they live in underground tunnels, like rats. They bite like rats. They steal like rats, they scare people like rats do, they stink like rats, they're wild like rats. Basically: there's a plague of rats that must be exterminated.

Jaume Joyce Araypuro: Sí, Mr. Inspector. Una plaga de rats.

Detective Inspector Thadeus: There are academic studies on the subject of violence praxis, but that's mere theory. We need to bring the theory to praxis.

Jaume Joyce Araypuro: Sí, señor, praxis.

Detective Inspector Thadeus: We need to catch them all. Lock them up in the appropriate institutions. Prisons, mental hospitals. Studies indicate that crime levels are sky high. Contemporary evil is not comparable with any prior era. We have to act quickly. We have no time to waste. No, hold on a sec. We won't do anything today, because I promised my wife I'd take her to the movies to see *The Maltese Falcon* by John Huston, goodbye.

Amanda Jane enters the parlor of the Palace of Versailles, radiant and happy, and with a proposal for her parents.

Amanda: Good morning, beloved father. Good morning, beloved mother. It's Sunday. The sun is shining and the birds are singing out all the virtues of living in a perfect world. I suggest we go have a picnic by the Antuvi River to celebrate the miracle of our marvelous family.

Mrs. Holofernes: If your father thinks it's a good idea, I'm all for it. Little Isabel II will also like the idea. Oh, it's been so long since we've done what more traditional families usually do when they do family things. I can't wait!

Amanda: Where would you like to go? What would you like to see? The river ducks? Or something else? The flamingos, perhaps?

Mrs. Holofernes: Your joie de vivre is inspirational, my dear daughter. I'm very happy for you. Your sudden happiness makes me and your father happy. My horoscope this morning was right: "Today you will have a marvelous day in the company of those you love most."

Amanda: Yeah, sure, but I'm talking about something else right now. I'm talking about a picnic. About doing what normal families do, the ones who love each other.

Father: Yes.

Mrs. Holofernes: Or no?

Amanda: Yes—let's go to the babbling brook.

Father: To the babbling brook, we can take the car.

Mrs. Holofernes: We could take a boat there.

Amanda: We can drive and then sail in a lovely boat.

Isabel II: Cood we bring Mollecule befor we have him put downe?

Amanda: We can do whatever we like.

Father: We can go there by boat.

Amanda: Yes, of course, we can do everything you'd like, Father, whatever you say.

Father: We can go in a lovely spick and span boat.

Amanda: Yes, of course, we can go there in a nice boat. We'll drive to the river and then we'll sail down, singing a popular song that we all know the words to.

Father: We'll take off our shirts and sandals and the tropical breeze will tousle our hair.

Mrs. Holofernes: We are a close family and we don't care about the future and we have no past to remember. We'll take photographs together like a nice family and then we'll post them on social media for everyone to see.

Amanda: Exactly. Basically we should celebrate that we're an adorable family and let our neighbors and the whole world know it, so we can keep up our good reputation as an adorable family. Look, there are flamingos by the river bank 🦩 I like their pink color.

Father: We'll go down to the river, we'll go down to the same river where our ancestors bathed. You will be sleeping and I will be awake listen to what I'm saying.

Mrs. Holofernes: We don't expect to find meaning in it all. Flamingos are pink. Pink is my favorite color. The color black is an absence I don't need in my life.

The Holofernes family arrives at the riverbank and sets up a picnic.

Amanda: The old nuclear power plants are silhouetted against the landscape. The trees die and the grass stopped growing long ago. We no longer remember what color it was. We swim through the polluted water, it is the red color of rancor.

Father: The day will come when there are no fathers left, no mothers left no left no flamingos left no recognizable music left.

Mrs. Holofernes: They'll be no houses left with pools or televisions nothing will be left but we will still swim through the polluted water of the Antuvi River. There will be no buildings left no cities no peoples but we will keep bathing in the river.

Amanda: (*whispering*) And then we will dine on the rotting flesh of humanity's cadavers.

Father: We'll trace invisible bridges through the clouds, so dead humanity can walk across.

Mrs. Holofernes: We have no future and we don't want to remember the past. We just want to go down to the river and swim among the flamingos. And that's why we are standing, now, beside this river. My horoscope this morning was right: "water will play an important role for you and your loved ones."

Father: Before there were people all around, swimming in the river, noshing in the meadows, carrying baskets filled with plums and other seasonal fruits. This tree, this river, they remind me of the fact that I am not a flamingo.

Amanda: (*whispering*) It's deceitful to put up with the flamingo's pink color.

Mrs. Holofernes: And the fluorescent lights that industrially replicate the summer sun.

Father: But the flamingos remind me of the fact of lying in a meadow filled with flowers with pink ponies and a rainbow, of everything that could be seen from there and everything that couldn't.

While the Holofernes family enjoys their picnic in one corner of the scene, Amanda sneaks off to another corner where Johnny waits, hidden. He has a pistol.

Johnny: Fuck, what are we doing? This is fucking bonkers. I'll go back to prison and you'll get locked up in a psychiatric hospital.

Amanda: Basically this is my last chance. Before we leave, before you and I disappear irreversibly. We have to do it now.

Johnny: I guess so.

Amanda: «I guess so»? What kind of reasoning is that?

Johnny: I can't think of anything more to tell you.

Amanda: Take out the pistol.

Johnny: Here you go. Your father's Smith & Wesson, perfectly clean and shiny, ready to be used.

Amanda: It's a very svelte pistol, a clean pistol, and emotive pistol. Come on, nothing to it but to do it.

Johnny and Amanda approach the Holofernes family, who sit on the grass beneath a large pine tree beside the river. Johnny carries the pistol in one hand. All the light is focused on the gleaming pistol, shiny as a freshly washed apple.

Amanda: As the eldest daughter of the Holofernes family, it is my duty to inform you that you are about to die.

Mrs. Holofernes: Calamity. Distrust. I don't know what to think of you, daughter of mine. Is this why you've brought us here? What are you doing with this man covered in tattoos who works rebuilding the stable? Are you having an affair? Are you in love? This looks very bad. I feel totally unsafe. Your father and I are very concerned.

Father: Very concerned.

Amanda: I'm in love with Johnny «el Vampir». He's an ex-addict, ex-con, ex-everything. But he has a heart as big as a mountain.

Mrs. Holofernes: You can't fall in love with a man like that, some delinquent you just met. You aren't even eighteen yet. And you're a Scorpio. Variable speeds, precipitations, transformations. I read in this magazine (*she waves the magazine repeatedly through the air*) that today Scorpios should not do anything, they shouldn't see anyone, they shouldn't even leave the house.

Amanda: Don't tell me what I can and cannot do, Mother. Fuck the zodiac.

Mrs. Holofernes: And you, mister ex-con ex-addict handyman: what do all those tattoos mean? What is your zodiac sign? What future do you want for my little daughter?

Johnny: These tattoos, ma'am, hide my sadness. I am the Exterminating Angel. I am the bubonic plague. I am the Vampiric Holocaust. Nothing ever grows again in my wake. I have fangs instead of human teeth. If I scratch at my skin you can see it coming off in clumps, rotting flesh, I stink of putrid cadaver. Some people think I have leprosy. My name is Evil.

Mother: My God . . . how gross. He is repugnant, Amanda. Why did you bring a leper to our picnic? Do you want us to get the plague? Quick, get him out of here! Call the doctor! I need to get a blood test!

Amanda: Johnny is a vampire, Mom, not a leper. He knows how to fight against God's destiny. He is a powerful demon.

Father: Nonsense! I only believe in the truth of religion, and then only maybe. These two have something up their sleeve. They are walking stealthily, silently, following the footsteps of their prey, like a band of hyenas in search of carrion, like the armed urban tribes from former industrial neighborhoods, an association of television savages destroying churches in the early eleventh century.

Amanda: You're right, Father. Johnny and I have a plan. To kill you right now. What do you think of that?

Mrs. Holofernes: Unseemly, Amanda. This whole thing is very unseemly.

Isabel II: An this ribber is frizing. Even da flamenkos ar gonn. Ebrything stincs of seamen, powder, and perverrsitdy.

Father: It's a punishment from God.

Mrs. Holofernes: Why are you speaking to us like this, Amanda? Why have you come with a tattooed man who threatens us with a pistol? Why do you torture us with your insanity?

Amanda: Don't be an idiot, Mom. (*She sings a song*): There's no mama / there's no papa / there's no woman / there's no friend / there's no forest / there's no sky / there's no oxygen / there's no shade / but there are flames, Mama / miniflames, Mama / that flare up and go out / they breathe and stretch / and polish the path / they festoon the retina / and sustain the structure / of fire and culture / where reality isn't always the norm / and words construct the form / our religion is the life we live / don't speak of normal lives / or neutral attitudes / all pure people disappear / within the structure of the empire / maintained by the blood and adultery / of our forefathers / too dead to be remembered / there's no mama / there's no papa / there's no woman / there's no friend / there's no forest / there's no sky / there's no oxygen / there's no shade / but there are flames, Mama / that flare up and go out / they breathe and stretch / and polish the path / that leads us to the firmament.

Mrs. Holofernes: I don't understand you, Amanda. We love you . . .

Amanda: That seemingly meaningless fragment is my confession, that I hate you—yes I hate and loathe this family. And I would like you, before you die, to confess all your crimes.

Father: I don't know what you're talking about, my dear.

Amanda: Yes you do. Your horrible crimes must not go unpunished. Shoot him, Johnny!

Johnny: He says he doesn't know what you're talking about.

Amanda: He's lying. He lies like a rug, Johnny. Shoot the gun!

Father: I am your creator. To you, I am God. I cannot die without first knowing what I am accused of. It wouldn't be fair.

Amanda: Life isn't fair, dear father. You created me and you destroyed me. And now you must pay. Everything in this life has a price. It doesn't matter if it's a fair price or not, this isn't the stock market on Wall Street. Wipe that useless smile off your face.

Mrs. Holofernes: The horoscope didn't say anything about all this, but it doesn't matter because now I'm standing in this meadow, waiting to be executed by my own daughter.

Amanda: And you, Mother, always looking the other way. Always hiding your head in the sand, like an ostrich. You will also pay, Mother, for not daring to report your sexually perverted husband. Shoot her, Johnny, shoot the dirty whore.

Johnny: She doesn't seem dangerous.

Amanda: You're wrong, my love. The most seemingly harmless people are the most perverse, sadistic and repugnant. Give me the pistol, Johnny, I'll do it myself. Bang-bang-bang-bang-bang-bang-bang-bang-bang-bang-bang-bang-bang-bang-bang-bang-bang-bang-bang-bang-bang-bang-bang-bang-bang-bang-bang-bang-bang-bang-bang-bang. Bang-bang-bang-bang-bang-bang-bang-bang-bang and . . . bang!

Mrs. Holofernes: The blood is sticky and makes me feel ephemeral in an ephemeral world. I'm bleeding out from the bullet that exploded my skull. Everything is hell.

Father: Yeah, I'm dying too. A bullet went through my esophagus. And it's strange, because lying here on the grass feels pretty good.

Mrs. Holofernes: There is a lot of light. It must be that tunnel everyone talks about.

Father: Stretched out in this improvised picnic, while my daughter murders me and cuts off my penis with scissors. Everything is red. Even the sky.

Isabel II: Oh all dis sticky blood. My parents r dying. Must I dye too? I had so much nasty shitt to do stil . . . I lost an ay from a straye bullet.

Amanda: Not you, Isabel II. You will live. I'm sorry about your eye but don't worry, you'll end up in a care home for minors—or something like that—and then you'll grow up, you'll work in a supermarket, and you'll fall in love with someone and you'll have kids and you'll be happy forevorandevermore, OK?

Isabel II: OK!

Amanda: Sometimes everything seems like a terrible joke. I study a lot, I read a lot, and I think I'm very intelligent, but really I have no fucking clue. It's unbearable. Unbearable. I hear the siren song, my Ulysses.

Johnny: Those are police sirens.

Amanda: Let's go, let's hide. The police are coming. Let's not let them catch us.

Johnny: I'll never let that happen.

Amanda: We need money. We can't flee without money. Nothing's free in this world, you know? Not even a toothbrush.

Johnny: Yes. I need a toothbrush.

Amanda: Let's go back to the house. We'll take my father's money. We'll be free and rich. In fact—exactly—we'll be rich so we can be free.

Johnny: Rich. Free. We'll buy hundreds of toothbrushes.

Johnny and Amanda Jane run off. Red and blue lights approach. Sirens. The barking of highly trained dogs. Blood. Picnic. A lost shoe. An open mouth. Large pools of blood. Four policemen and Detective Inspector Thadeus.

Detective Inspector Thadeus: This is outrageous. A shameful sight. Take this girl out of here. And put a safety cordon up before the guys from *The Bronx Messenger* show up to take photos of this butchery for tomorrow's front page.

Policeman no. 1: The Holofernes family, one of the richest in the Valley of the Bronx.

Policeman no. 2: It wasn't a red herring. Everything that mestizo told us is coming true. This is a massacre.

Detective Inspector Thadeus: Opinions are just opinions until proven otherwise. When the poor can't stand the rich's impertinence, he destroys him. It's normal. I've arrested people who traffick with children. I've locked up people who sold human organs, people who steal wool, serial killers. Blood and guts.

Policeman no. 1: Blood & guts.

Policeman no. 2: A massacre of the rich by the proletariat class. Typical.

Detective Inspector Thadeus: Blessed be the thieves and the murderers! Blessed be all the defenseless who seek a guilty party for the disgrace of humanity! They've done X-rays on the fat rolls of the woman who massages destroyed genitals, they've invented geometric chants to scare off ghosts. Blessed be all the defenseless! Blessed be the anti-depressives, too! Blessed be all the brotherhoods of losers, because only they shall inherit the earth after the dinosaurs! 🦕

Policeman no. 1: Forensic analysis: two cadavers, a man, a middle-aged woman, and one survivor, a twelve-year-old girl, and a lap dog.

Policeman no. 2: Forensic analysis: Mr. and Mrs. Holofernes. Family.

Detective Inspector Thadeus: Forensic analysis: one pistol, a lot of bullets. The first bullet struck the man's lung (side note: his virile member is also chopped up).

Policeman no. 1: The second bullet entered the woman's face, frontally.

Policeman no. 2: The third bullet was headed for the woman but hit a tree, bounced, and took out the eye of the little girl.

Detective Inspector Thadeus: The fourth bullet destroyed the man's testicles, went straight through them and landed in the woman's foot.

Policeman no. 1: The fifth bullet didn't hit anyone, it flew far, far from here and killed a flamingo who was levitating tranquilly over the river.

Policeman no. 2: The sixth bullet entered the woman's thorax, exited her body, ricocheted off a rock, and hit the man's mouth.

Detective Inspector Thadeus: The seventh bullet exploded the woman's head.

Policeman no. 1: I don't know where the eighth bullet is.

Policeman no. 2: The ninth bullet traveled like a ray of cosmic light through the contact lens in the woman's eye.

Detective Inspector Thadeus: The tenth bullet made a pronounced veer to the right, in every sense.

Policeman no. 1: The eleventh bullet got lost in a black hole.

Policeman no. 2: The twelfth bullet is lodged in the man's skull.

Detective Inspector Thadeus: The thirteenth bullet perforated a perfectly structured esophagus.

Policeman no. 1: The fourteenth bullet imitated the sound of a trombone.

Policeman no. 2: The fifteenth bullet set sail for the new world.

Detective Inspector Thadeus: The sixteenth bullet measured faith in centimeters and weighed the soul in kilograms.

Policeman no. 1: The seventeenth bullet didn't want to kill anyone.

Policeman no. 2: The eighteenth bullet had a more personal, intimate tone.

Detective Inspector Thadeus: The nineteenth bullet flew like a plane and landed on a desert island.

Policeman no. 1: The twentieth bullet flew over the sun and navigated the universe in zero gravity.

Policeman no. 2: The twenty-first bullet was as out of tune as a parade band.

Detective Inspector Thadeus: The twenty-second bullet was in a big hurry.

Policeman no. 1: The twenty-third bullet lives in a lung and is very content there.

Policeman no. 2: The twenty-fourth bullet went on a beach vacation.

Detective Inspector Thadeus: The twenty-fifth bullet was fair and loyal.

Policeman no. 1: The twenty-sixth bullet arrived at the expected time, punctually.

Policeman no. 2: The twenty-seventh bullet made a perfect arc.

Policeman no. 1: The twenty-eight bullet . . .

Policeman no. 2: The twenty-ninth . . .

Detective Inspector Thadeus: That's enough! Case closed. There aren't many mysteries to solve here, no complicated plots. This isn't a detective novel. It is what it is: a simple murder. People die in the stupidest ways you can imagine. I've seen catheters, UTIs, black vomit, sleds pointed into the void. Nothing that hasn't been seen before (and now I'll smoke a cigarette).

Policeman no. 1: Where are the murderers, Inspector?

Detective Inspector Thadeus: I'm convinced they've returned to the Holofernes house. A murderer never flees without his toothbrush. Let's go.

Meanwhile, Johnny and Amanda arrive at the Palace of Versailles and head up to her father's office to get the money out of the safe.

Johnny: We gotta blow this pop stand before the cops show up.

Amanda: We could go to Madagascar, or Sebastopol. I'll let my finger fall on a map of the world, and we'll go wherever it lands. Otherwise I'd rather stay here with you forevermore, in this precise instant that could very well be a dream that lasts forevermore, where everything is fresh and pretty, where everything is innocent like a field of sunflowers; we will try to look at each other tenderly, we will try to smile forgetting all the darkness as if our faces were buried behind a mask of kindness and we have our whole lives ahead of us filled with things to experience together without leaving this room.

Johnny: Hush now. Don't get corny. Look, a shadow in the shadow of the door.

Amanda: The shadow knows us. The shadow follows us. The shadow knows everything.

KingKong of the Bronx makes a simian jump through the doorway.

KingKong: Uh-uh!

Johnny: Whatdafuck are you doing here.

KingKong: Hello, Johnny Dynamite. I heard the sirens of the police cars. You know why the cops came so fast, don't you, Johnny boy? Our friend Jaume Joyce Araypuro ratted you out. Uh-uh!

Johnny: Shit.

KingKong: It doesn't matter. By this point the cops must have found the bodies. They'll be here before too long. I can already hear the sirens and the barking of the highly trained dogs. You got yourself a real hot tamale, I'll admit it, but I don't envy you. This girl will only bring you problems but do what you want. As for me, I only want Ole Man Holofernes's cash. I heard you talking and I know he keeps it here, in a safe.

Amanda: There's no safe here.

KingKong: Johnny, tell your little hussy that if she doesn't tell me where the safe is I'll kill her. I'll kill you both. You and your lady who looks like a carpet muncher. Uh-uh!

Johnny: No she doesn't. She's a sensational chick. Leave her alone.

Amanda: I don't need a man to defend me (*to Johnny*), and I'm no carpet muncher (*to KingKong*). I like cock as much as you do. You wanted to be a gorilla but you're nothing more than a chimpanzee. I'm sure behind bars you were sucking dick nonstop. I'm sure you brushed your teeth with the semen of your HIV-positive fellow inmates. Am I wrong? I'm sure you're one of those bastards who goes around infecting every hole in reach with AIDS, aren't you?

KingKong: Where's the safe?

Amanda: I told you there is no safe, my father kept his money in the bank, like everyone does.

KingKong: You're lying. You're a fucking liar. If you don't tell me where the old man kept his cash I'll kill you right here, I'll kill you both.

Amanda: OK, OK. It's true, I was lying. I thought I could trick you but obviously I'm a bad liar, I mean I'd like to know how to lie like a professional liar, I'd like to be a real expert in the art of lying, get a degree in lying to know all the ins and outs, write a doctoral thesis on lies, be invited to international symposia to discuss the lie. But, obviously, I don't know how to lie. The safe is in the parlor downstairs.

Amanda Jane, KingKong, and Johnny head down the stairs toward the parlor. Amanda, who is walking behind them both, pulls out the pistol and shoots KingKong from behind.

KingKong: A bullet went through my skull. It's nice to be a son of a bitch. You both tricked me.

Amanda: No one fucks with me, and no one slags me off.

KingKong: I'm dying. I had a great future ahead of me and a lot of plans. I wanted to study numismatics. Get a degree in Sucrology, Nymphology, and Trapology at the University of Saint Jeremias. Open a fishing tackle store. Start a stamp collection. I wanted to be rich and forget about all the prejudices against bald people, I wanted to be like King Kong and climb the Empire State Building with my beloved Queen Kong and ask for her hand in marriage. Uh-uh!

Amanda: Well you done fucked that up. And besides, there's no safe here, you idiot. The money is in a shoebox, old school.

Johnny: You watch too many movies, Mr. King. Bang-bang-bang.

KingKong falls to the floor, dead. Red and blue lights draw closer. Sirens. The barking of highly trained dogs. The police surround the Holofernes home armed with rifles. Detective Inspector Thadeus picks up a megaphone.

Detective Inspector Thadeus: «Attention. Attention. Biiiiiiip! (*the megaphone isn't working very well*) Piece of shit . . . Attention, this is Commissioner Thadeus Olivera. We know your names: Johnny Dynamite and Amanda Jane. Those are two acceptable names. We know you are inside the house. We know the house has two floors. We know that you are on one of the two floors. We know that the house has a modern design, despite being a kitschy imitation of the Palace of Versailles. We know that the two floors are connected by a staircase. We know that staircases don't always lead people to where they'd like to go. People can be so maniacal. We know that expectations can't always be met. We know that your expectation is to leave this house alive and be free. We can only promise the first option. The first option requires a series of legal regulations that you will have to meet. We know that laws are not always just. Justice is a fiction. We know that . . .»

Johnny: (*shouting from a window of the house*) We don't want to turn ourselves in. We have a great future ahead of us.

Amanda: Howl, howl, howl.

Johnny: What the hell was that about?

Amanda: We are murderers, my love. There is no turning back. We are fugitives from justice, like Bonny & Clide . . . ! I have the revolver. I'm invincible. Bang-bang.

Detective Inspector Thadeus: Girl with tiger-like eyes is shooting at us from inside the house. The car windows are shattering. A bullet perforates my nose and I can no longer sniff out crime.
Policeman no. 1: A bullet goes through my honest policeman's heart.
Policeman no. 2: Sir, I believe a bullet has also hit my stomach, but I was a corrupt policeman. I dealt impounded drugs and ran a prostitution ring. Now I can die in peace.
Detective Inspector Thadeus: You're right. You're covered in blood. Both of you are dead. Clinically dead. Sorry, boys. No one ever said this was an easy job. I see things like this every day. And now I'll smoke a cigarette, even though I can't smell it.

Amanda and Johnny escape through the house's back door and into the woods, disappearing among the trees.

Amanda: I hit him, Johnny my dear . . . hit and sunk him! We're free!
Johnny: Let's hightail it out of here before more cops arrive. They'll fry us in the electric chair! Let's head up the mountain, hide in the darkness of the trees and take full advantage of this moonless night.
Amanda: It was on nights like this that ☠☠☠ showed up to abuse me.
Johnny: Your father is dead. He can't hurt you anymore.
Amanda: The shadow is following us. The shadow knows everything.
Johnny: What the actual fuck are you talking about?

Meanwhile a limping figure appears amid the trees. It is Javier Holofernes who has risen from the dead. His face is pale and his entrails emerge from the bullet holes in his body. He has become one of the undead.

Amanda: Holyfuck, my father turned into a zombie!
Johnny: Excuse me, what's that you say . . . ?
Amanda: A zombie, dear Johnny, one of the undead. Zombies act by night and with nasty intent. If they bite you, you turn into one of them.

Johnny: Like vampires?

Amanda: More or less.

Johnny: Can they die?

Amanda: Yes, but only if you destroy their brains. Here comes my un-father.

Father: Dear daughter, you killed me, yes, but you didn't kill me enough. And now I've come back from the dead to take my revenge. I'll eat you and your tattooed junkie boyfriend and no one can stop me.

Amanda: Not a chance, dear Dad. You were disgusting before, but this is next level. Your eye is hanging out.

Father: Let me devour you, my girl, like in that painting by Goya, *Saturn Devouring His Son*. That way you'll always be with me.

Amanda: Not a chance, Dad. You abused me throughout my entire childhood and adolescence and you're still messing with me after death? Not a chance.

Amanda pounces on her zombie father and starts hitting his head with the butt of her revolver. She hits him and hits him and hits him, staining her whole body with black blood. She hits him until his skull explodes. She hits him until there's nothing left of his face. She hits him until there's nothing left of her father.

Johnny: Ugh. What carnage. You took it all out on your old dad, huh?

Amanda: Well, yeah, haha. Fucking parents, so gross, they're a trauma that hunts you down like a ghost from the past and then you spend half your life paying a psychologist or, even worse, a psychoanalyst. Anyhoo, where are we going now, Johnny my dear? I'll remind you that the cops are on our trail.

Johnny: We'll run off. We'll hide in a motel tonight and tomorrow we'll rob a car and drive far away from here. Put on this blonde wig and these fake hipster glasses so they don't recognize you.

Amanda: OK. Let's go. Let's run. We'll go by foot, yes, we'll go by foot along the darkest path of them all at a quarter to midnight as if we were crossing hyperbolic galaxies, completely suspicious, and the foreigners will stone us from their balconies and we will decide international wars and we'll be too old to stand the crickets breaking the silence of the night and we'll lift bottles of wine as if they were synchronized swimming trophies and we will toast to what's important and what isn't and then we'll find it all pretty relative and we'll learn to talk to the birds, we'll do all that and always in this order of importance. Where are we, Johnny my dear?

Johnny: I'm lost. I thought I knew where I was going and that there was a hotel nearby, but I'm lost.

Amanda: The watch hands buck up at this hour of the day. Stars and meteorites fall on the Valley of the Bronx. These shoes hurt my feet.

Johnny: Take them off then.

Amanda: Oh, Johnny, what do we do now? I mean, we can't spend our lives walking around lost, or can we? These trees and their shadows are pretty depressing. Where will we sleep?

Johnny: Not a clue.

Amanda: We'll live each day in a different city. I'll become a prostitute and you'll be my pimp and protect me from abusive johns. We'll found a new religion and become millionaires. We'll travel all over the world and learn every language (everyone knows Lucifer is a polyglot). We'll have a garden with no flowers and a house with no roof. We'll be vampires in the eternal night.

Johnny: Stop with all the baloney already.

Amanda: Who will love life when I'm no longer around, Johnny?

Johnny: You never shut up, do you?

Amanda: No. Everyone always tells me I talk too much. Do you think I talk too much?

Johnny: No.

Amanda: Yes. Yes you do think that but I don't give a shit, you know? You think my legs are hairy? I haven't waxed for centuries, but I forbid you to mention it or I can accuse you of mansplaining and you won't like that one bit. Ohmygod, I think I'm getting a zit on my face. So gross, I must look horrible. I'm sure you don't want me anymore. Do you still want me, Johnny my dear?

Johnny: Yes. Look, we're already at the motel. Neon lights. Silent parked cars. We'll get a room with a big bed and a television.

Amanda: I don't like this place. It's dirty. It's, like, impersonal. There are stains on the carpet that could be blood, or semen.

Johnny: The room is cheap. It'll do for today. It is in this particular time between day and night that you and I find ourselves in this room. And it is a totally impersonal room: the bed impeccably made, the disgusting ochre carpet, a tacky still-life painting on the wall, cable television, white curtains, a window that looks out on the black of night, a sensation of anonymity, everything is horribly impersonal; I mean the room isn't exactly a suite but it'll do.

Amanda: You're right, my dear. The important thing is that we're here, you and I, looking at each other the way only two lovers could, holding hands with our fingers touching the way only two lovers could. Relax, there's no need for words, no need to speak much in the precise instant that very well could be a dream that lasts forevermore. Even though I'm sure you'll soon tire of me anyway, like I've already grown tired of you. You don't know me from Eve, you know nothing about me. And I know nothing about you, truth be told. In fact, I only wanted to use you.

Johnny: You talk too much. We'll sleep in this motel tonight, and tomorrow we'll go somewhere else.

Amanda: You men are only good for doing the dirty work. Mere pack animals.

Johnny: Stop being silly and put on your PJs.

Amanda: I fall in love with someone different every day.

Johnny: That's a lot of work. Go on, brush your teeth.

Amanda: Mediocrity is the servant of evil. Forget the savage darkness. Exactly, as if the world were nothing more than an enormous schoolyard.

My heart is terrified but my brain feels free. Everything seems marvelous. I want to forget myself, forget nausea. Quit being a slave and become a master.

Johnny: Be quiet for a little while and let me watch the news, do you mind? They're talking about us. They'll fry us in the electric chair if they catch us.

Amanda: Don't tell me to be quiet, Johnny. Oh, why can't the world be more neat and tidy? I suffer over the most trivial things. What will happen to the rancid carpet in this motel when they change it? And those fake flowers, why are they just there and not a little to the left? Some days I cry for no reason. But it rarely affects me. I wish things would affect me more.

Johnny: You are so annoying. If you don't shut up, I'm gonna bitch slap you.

Amanda: Silence is fake, just like this blonde wig I'm wearing. Appearances are deceiving. We live in a world filled with violence and, to be specific, male violence. I have to kill all these bastards . . .

Johnny: What the fuck are you talking about now?

Amanda: I am talking about how everything is filled with masters who subjugate and subjugated slaves.

Johnny: Why are you pointing that gun at me? Mandy . . . put down the gun . . . what . . . are you doing?

Amanda: «Sleapbdeabbeaffedbeapleafbed!».

Johnny: What's that you say?

Amanda: «sleapbdeabbeaffedbeapleafbed! sleapbdeabb! sleaphffedbeap le!sleapbdeabb!sleapbdeabbeaffedbeapleafbed! sleapbdeabb! sleaphffed beaple!sleapbdeabb!sleapbdeabbeaffedbeapleafbed! sleapbdeabb! slea- phffedbeaple!sleapbdeabb!sleapbdeabbeaffedbeapleafbed! sleapbdeabb! sleaphffedbeaple!sleapbdeabb!sleapbdeabbeaffedbeapleafbed! sleapbdeabb! sleaphffedbeaple!sleapbdeabb!sleapbdeabbeaffedbeapleaf- bed! sleapbdeabb! sleaphffedbeaple!sleapbdeabb!sleapbdeabbeaffedbea pleafbed! sleapbdeabb!»

THE FAKE MUSE - 135

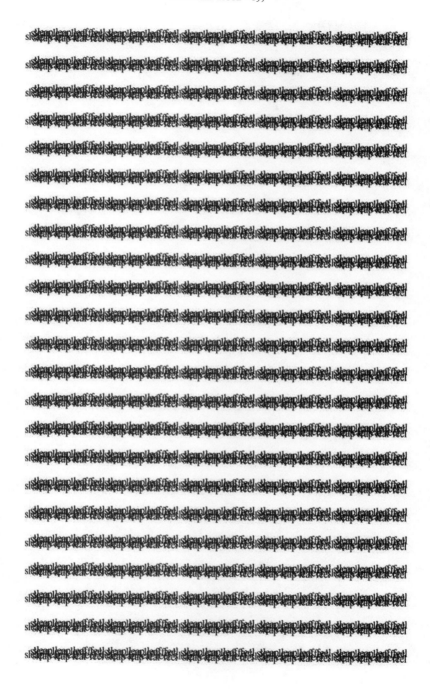

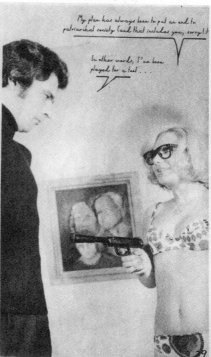

Johnny falls to the ground, dead. Applause is heard. More applause. Even more applause. The curtain goes down.

The Fake Muse

Mandyjane rolls into the middle of the room like a hurricane, drops the still smoking gun (the smoke draws a skull in the air ☠) onto the table, and, after sighing dramatically, she waves to the man she's come to interview, who sits and waits chainsmoking Almogàvers™ cigarettes and reading *The Bronx Messenger*'s articles about the crime wave battering the region. Then they both are still for a while, almost as if in a black and white photograph, or perhaps like two statues swathed in cold marble.

"OK, can we get started? I'm a specialist in wasting time . . . which is why I have no time to waste. What's your first question?"

"Ah, yes, of course. Forgive me. I have all the questions prepared in a notebook. One second while I get out my tape recorder and . . ."

"No. No tape recorders."

"You don't want . . ."

"No. I don't want. In fact, I'd prefer you'd sent me the questions in writing. I prefer to write the responses myself. I'd also like to know why you're carrying a smoking gun as if you just shot someone."

"The responses. Very well. Why are you looking at me like that? Don't you like guns? I thought men liked them, it's a very phallic symbol, don't you think?"

"Phallic? I don't know. As for the responses, yes, I prefer—exactly—I prefer to write the responses down myself, because otherwise people print whatever they feel like. The words must be as precise as clockwork, do you understand?"

"Yes, of course I understand. I understand perfectly. But since I'm already here I'll ask you the questions I've prepared, if you don't mind. The first question I wanted to ask you is the following: What's a writer like you doing in a place like this?"

"I don't know what I'm doing here, or how I got here. I thought I knew but I can't remember. I live in a primitive state of neurotic irresponsibility."

"Don't worry about that. Seriously, for God's sake, don't worry. Who are you hoping to please, or who is your potential audience?"

"I only write to please myself."

"Sure, obviously. I wanted to know why you quit writing. People say you're a hermit now. You don't show up on the radar at all."

"Excuse me, what did you just say? I was dreaming. There was a flamingo in my dream."

"Flamingo. OK. Would you say you're a hermit?"

"Mmmh, no. I wouldn't say that. I would never say that. Hermits don't explain themselves. They disappear when they feel like it and that's that. In any case these jibbery-jabbery questions are attacking my immune system. Is it really important to know about a writer's private life? Your questions seem . . . they seem totally pornographic. Yes, that's the word: pornographic."

"Sorry . . . I didn't want . . ."

"You didn't want, but you ask anyway."

"I ask anyway. Whoa, it's true. Forgive me."

After that, they both remain in silence for a few seconds. Mandyjane is sitting in the chair in a posture like something out of a novel by Sacher-Masoch. She's dressed in super short shorts and a sophisticated ivory-colored T-shirt that makes her seem even younger than she is; or at least as young as a girl almost eighteen can be, despite her feeling—to quote her own words—like "a three-hundred-year-old granny trapped in a postpubescent body."

"I didn't want to offend you, but I'd prefer it if you didn't describe me. Any and all descriptions in the twenty-first century are offensive. And people. People are constantly describing themselves in selfies, but really they flee their own shadows."

"Are you talking about the magic world of social media?"

"I'm not familiar with it. The cyberworld seems like a very distant place."

"That's understandable."

"What's the weather like outside? Is it bad or not? Is it raining or what?"

"It's a sunny day, a marvelous day. Stunning. Unprecedented. On the radio they said this will probably be the hottest summer ever, with temperatures of more than 104, which could transform the entire Valley of the Bronx into a huge ice cream that then melts into some sort of really disgusting dark and rotten liquid that could become an I.B.M. that lays waste to everything."

"I.B.M.? What's that?"

"An Immense Ball of Mucus, like the one that swept over the campus of the University of Saint Jeremias a few years ago. It was in all the papers."

"Aha. Well, here, inside this room, the air is quite breathable, thanks to the enormous fans hanging from the ceiling that oscilate constantly, so much so that I get dizzy if I look up at them for too long, as if the entire universe were spinning around me."

"Of course, I understand perfectly. Those fans remind me of when I was a little girl and went to the supermarket with my mom and there were all these fans, and I walked majestically between those purple and black fruits. And pink and yellow. Flies flew around them like they were rotting corpses."

"The artificial light in supermarkets is deceiving, it doesn't allow us to think calmly but it industrially replicates the summer sun. That's why decent people no longer live in cities. They kneel between the forest's trees and become rocks."

"Rocks. OK. Can I ask you what's your marvelous technique for approaching literary language?"

"Words have shadows. But the sun also rises, sometimes."

"What is your opinion of contemporary literature?"

"Despite what you may think, I always judge the inside of a book by its cover. And now, let me ask you a question: Do you mind telling me who you are?"

"I am . . . I am a journalist from a literary magazine. We agreed to meet today for this interview. Don't you remember?"

"No."

"That's okay, don't worry about it. Our magazine features unpublished writers, with the only conditions that they are under thirty years old and have committed a crime. It is a magazine with a single issue devoted to murder in fiction. We went bankrupt making it."

"Ah, very well. And what sort of writing do you publish?"

"All kinds, we publish all kinds. There's a story about a man obsessed with his baldness who, after inventing a magic formula, turns into an ultrahairy gorilla. There are other stories, too, about cannibal vampires at the movies, mutant hamsters, extraterrestrials, Nazi sects, mentally ill pedophiles, people who seemingly have a happy life and wear the masks of model citizens but who, deep down, want to experience catharsis and boldfacedly practice EVIL to set themselves free."

"That's normal. The excessive rules and codes in a hypercontrolled society like ours can only lead to this sort of psychotic behavior that exceeds all morals, all ethics. In fact, the blame lies with the dictatorship of language, the primary invisible oppressor."

"Of course. About that . . . what advice would you give someone who wants to be a writer?"

"There is no advice cheap enough for the eyes that look at the world."

"You really have no advice to give?"

"Well . . . if pedants drive you nuts, if social climbers nauseate you, if trends make you constipated, if you're horrified by false prophets, if you're shocked by sect followers and (finally) if you find reality boring, you'd be better off becoming a visual artist."

"Aha. Any other lessons, please?"

Lesson 1: Be impersonal
Lesson 2: Be obscure
Lesson 3: Be pompous
Lesson 4: Be serious
Lesson 5: Be unintelligible

"Unintelligible. Very good."

"Be repetitive. Incorrect. Awkward. Strange. Loveable. Ugly. Idiotic."

"Idiotic. Perfect."

"Be inconveniently boring, a karaoker of texts, an emphatic prankster, ungainly, an accused repeater

a countryless citizen
an ecstatic xenophile

                                   a passive-aggressive thumbtack pusher

a first-class instigator

                                   an antipretentious gourmet flowerdeflowerer

a great disappearer

                                             a vampirized busybody

a shower dancer

                                   a wings and thigh shaker

an impertinent criticizer

                                             a silence resister

a reckless knife sharpener

                                             a midnight vagabond or a dawn risker

a snoring machine

                                             an intentionally inept professional

a mercurial improvisor

                                             an Olympic champion of summer naps

highly disorganized

                                                       . . . obsessively imperfect."

"Imperfect. Very good. What message do you want to convey to your readers?"

"None at all. People hope to have illuminations while picking their noses or going to music festivals to rockandroll their asses off or get a stiff neck or while buying new sneakers or doing whatever and, meanwhile, they run up and down and all around like lit flames filled with pain . . ."

"Do you like to complain?"

"Yes. It's my favorite sport. But, believe me, I'd rather not do it. I'd prefer to live in a world where people were truly honest and I didn't have to waste time complaining."

"But . . . that's impossible!"

"Exactly. Impossible. Modern life seems to consist in screwing others to get to the top, like an obstacle race. All our education consists in programming ourselves to be authentic sharks willing to devour each other."

At this point in the interview, the young woman scratches her leg nervously. Despite first appearances, it is actually a strong, muscular leg, likely of German provenance, a leg prepared to scale any large mountain, to reach any peak inaccessible to mere mortals (expect, perhaps, a yeti).

"If you don't mind, let's get back to the interview: Do you write to understand yourself better?"

"I'm not my fictional story just the same way I'm not my grocery list."

"I'd love it if you signed a book for me. What do you think about signing books?"

"Look, I shouldn't say this . . . but I will: people who want their favorite authors to sign books are despicable. I mean, if a book's already filled with letters, why should we add more? It makes no sense. Now I only write dedications (and I sign with an X, like the illiterate do) of this sort:

> *You'd be better off doing crosswords,*
> *At least you'd learn something*
> *Signed*
> *X*

Or like this, for example:

> *Who are you? What do you want from me?*
> *Do we even know each other?*
> *Signed*
> *X*

"Very nice. Lovely. Marvelous."

"I still don't understand what you're doing here, and with a smoking gun."

"Don't worry. The important thing is that we're here, you and I, looking at each other as only two strangers could."

"What don't I need to worry about? What do you mean?"

"I mean that now I understand everything. It is words that brought us to this situation. Our incomplete brains have completed each other thanks to words! Don't you see we're made for each other?"

"No. I don't see it. Excuse me, but I don't know you at all. I'd say you're a bit confused."

"You're wrong. It sounds happy. It sounds empirical. Our children demand to be conceived!"

"Look, young lady, I don't want to have children with you . . . I don't know you at all!"

"Why not? Why not, huh? We will try to always look at each other tenderly, we will try to smile forgetting all the darkness as if our faces were buried behind a mask of kindness and we have our whole lives ahead of us filled with beautiful things to experience together."

"Cut it out. I demand to know who you are and why you have that pistol. Are you a criminal? I should call the police . . ."

"Oh, don't be so boring! There's nothing worse in this life than being boring! Sometimes I have the feeling that our entire life is written out in advance by a capricious demiurge, like a novel but with no beginning, climax, or resolution or anything like that."

When she says the word "novel," the young woman grows suddenly quiet. She looks at her notebook. There's nothing written in it. She is now still, like frozen, like petrified. The man says:

"Stop it! No more stories! What are you talking about? In fact . . . I would like to know the reason behind your visit, young lady. I mean the real reason. I know you didn't come here just to interview me. I can tell. But what is your motive? Do we know? Should it be revealed now? If not, what then? Later? Later, when? Where did you come from? Who are you? Why are you here? And your name? Should we say it? Do we know it? Or what?"

"On my passport it says Amanda Jane Holofernes. But I'm not Amanda or Holofernes anymore. Finito. I rename myself Mandyjane Deathlove. I resist control. I place all my eggs in the basket of imagination, excess, the mystical, the irrational. I explode all my inner worlds as if there were no judgement day, no truth and no lies. Now I can transcend the historical and patriarchal limitations of my natural fictional condition, and divert the recursive structures of my thoughts of my traumatic past."

"I don't comprehend . . ."

"You don't get it yet? You designed me as a woman in your stupid violent fiction, but I redesigned myself as a posthuman being, filled with new codes, murmurs, and secret plots to emancipate myself from your diabolical plot. I am reborn Mandyjane Deathlove, destroyer of worlds, queen of the vampires, First Lady of a new race of superior beings."

"No . . . I don't understand any of what you're saying but I wish you the best, Miss Mandyjane, really I do. I hope you can fulfill all your dreams and that you'll be very happy. I'm sure you will. All you need to do is roll up your sleeves and give it your best, which I'm convinced is a lot. You can do incredible things and I have every faith in you, because I think you're an incredible and marvelous being, full of energy and intelligence. You are incredible and genius in every sense of the word and I fully trust that you can accomplish everything you set ou—"

"Shut up for once! You sound like a damn horoscope! I can't stand condescension! And wipe that stupid smile off your face!"

"You . . . you're insane!"

"Relax, don't lose your cool. Calm down. Control your sphincters."

"I can't relax! You can't show up like this at my house and shout at me this way. What . . . what does this whole story mean?"

"You don't understand? What part don't you understand? We live in another dimension here."

"What in the sam hill are you talking about?"

"I exist now and here because you are imagining me and I am imagining you. I am behind the observer, observing the observer."

The man frowns probingly. Beads of sweat slip down his forehead. He hesitates. He stammers. He pulls back.

"I don't understand any of this byzantine circumlocution . . . who are you really?"

"I can be whatever you want me to be or I can be absolutely nothing. Singularity is deceptive. Everything can be divided by itself. I'm a mutant hamster, a vampire, and king kong; I'm a stranger and I'm your best friend; I'm the green tree of life or the Exterminating Angel. Paranoid subject, man who pretends to be a woman, woman who pretends to be a girl, girl who becomes God, templar knight, astronaut, and criminal. I am the image destined to be devoured and processed by the honest intestines of the author."

"Mmmh, sounds complicated."

"It's not. Our story is a book where the pages keep getting turned again and again until in the end there are no more and everything disappears."

"These statements are anti-Aristotelian and not very empirical. I can't put up with this. Leave, please. I've had enough of little questions and impertinent statements for today!"

"And I'm totally over your frankensteinization imposed on my persona. You imagined or invented me with an absolutely normative body and forced me to be sexually assaulted by my own father, and to become a hysterical and merciless killer, repeating all the clichés of 'abused-woman-seeks-revenge,' as if there were no laws in place and the only solution was going around *shooting* people! And, as if that weren't enough, you made me come here to do this stupid interview just to play the author part and act like a little genius and on top of it all you start complaining? It's pathetic!"

"OK, maybe you have a point . . . but just a little while ago you said you wanted to have my children! What a contradiction!"

"Hahahah! Do you really think a hottie like me would fall in love with a has-been like you? Guys are all the same. They promise to love you forever and ten minutes later they're cheating on you with the first woman they see with six tits, four feet, and seven eyes and they get all heated up like a rotisserie chicken!"

"There is no greater disgrace than the disdain of the muses . . ."

"Your muse, me?? Haha! That's a good one! If anything, it's you who's my muse! I used you, chewed you up like a piece of gum and spit you out into this book! I'm here to make you see that, no matter how much you love your creations, you can't try to control them."

"I can't? If this is one of my novels and you are nothing more than a phantasmal projection of my mind, then I'm the one who decides when and how this interview and this book end."

"I don't agree. You exist only as long as your characters believe in you, not the other way around. Understand?"

"What sort of horrific Pirandellian dialectic is this? I am Lord and Master of all my creations, legally and emotionally. I have the power!"

"HAHAHAHAHAHA! Typical behavior of a pathetic m.c. pig. What exactly is power? When a person represents everyone's will, that is power. But if this 'everyone' is merely fictional beings, what real power can be exercised?"

"Get out of my house."

"This isn't your house."

"Where am I? What is this place?"

"This is a place where they bring people with incomplete brains."

"This is unnecessary. I need my medicine and for everything to make sense!"

"Unmake yourself. Your mental muddle is the one playing these demiurgical games. You want to dominate and possess your muses, instead of serving and adoring them. Your concept of art contains large doses of abnegation, abjection, and slavery."

"That's a big lie! None of this makes any sense. Your words are utterly nonsensical . . ."

"Shut up for once and don't lose the thread . . . stop thinking of dumb stuff and focus on the plot! Where do you want to end up? Where did all this start? Rewrite! That's an order! And then I'll decide what to do with you!"

"Yes, okay . . . Amanda . . . no, Mandy—exactly—Mandyjane is in the middle of the street with a smoking gun in her hands, her gaze lost on the pure contemplation of something still unnamed. A group of kids run by her shrieking and laughing. For a moment, she realizes that this scene could last forever and that she would be happy for ever and ever. It could all be about that precise instant, with the kids shrieking and all, but describing it would require millions of words. Maybe some other time. No. There won't be another time. The time has to be now. It has to be right now. The kids are all dressed the same, in gray jackets and trousers, white shirts and red ties. They must go to one of those extremely expensive private schools. Fresh, radiant faces; red cheeks, happy smiles. An ambulance drives down the street, its siren wailing. She pays it no mind. She simply stands, planted in that street lined with pretty houses. The neighborhood is one of those pretentious, boring upper-class neighborhoods, where plastic people live, trying to stay young by vampirizing each other. The ambulances drive fast, too fast, searching for a finish line when there is no path. Mandyjane reaches a Victorian-style door. The entire house is a tacky reproduction of the Palace of Versailles. She rings the doorbell. From inside approaching footsteps are heard. The door opens and she enters the house. She walks through a hall, over a carpet covered in mites and suspicious stains. Finally, she reaches the parlor. She rolls into the middle of the room like a hurricane, drops the still smoking gun onto the table and, after sighing dramatically, she waves to the man she's come to interview, who sits and waits chainsmoking Almogàvers™ cigarettes. Then they are both still for a while, almost as if in a black and white photograph, or perhaps like two statues swathed in cold marble. Everything is repetition. Nausea. Signs. Rumors. Visions. Everything is blurry . . . I observe Mandyjane's sky-blue eyes that contain a thousand hallelujahs in their iridescent irises. We don't believe in the past. Memory is a wife who cheats on you. Only what I am writing at this moment makes sense, the rest is unreal. The story ends. Then do whatever you want: walk the dog, call one of your girlfriends, maybe go to the movies, whatever . . . Keep writing. The door to the Victorian house opens, Mandyjane enters decisively. She walks along a red carpet filled with entire civilizations of bacteria invisible to the human eye and then she goes into the parlor, which is bursting with a gloomy silence. Before that, there was nothing more than an uninterrupted murmur of sighs that just dissipated into the ether. He serves hot coffee. A thread of steam emerges from the mug that she stirs with a spoon. The liquid moves concentrically. Prediction of uncertain futures. Her hand picks up a lit cigarrette from the ashtray and brings it to her red-lipsticked lips. Why has she come? What will be her first words? Is she neurasthenic? Perhaps, but the social atmosphere also plays a part. Everything is theater. The young woman has brought a book with her. It is one of my books. She asks me to sign it for her. I hate signing books! Ah, fake muse sitting here, with your long black hair, looking at me . . . no, even worse, scrutinizing me with your sky-blue eyes as if conducting a life-or-death interrogation. What exactly do you want? Are you seeking the meaning of your existence? I'm not a guru! Why aren't you saying anything? Speak . . . ! Say something, for the love of God! What is it you want from me? Do you want me to rip out my tongue? Or what? Aha, I know what you want. You want me to give you all the power so the corneas of the volcanoes in everyone's eyes explode, so there is no more cheap advice, is that it, adorable reader? Is that it? . . . OK, OK, I'll give you all the power . . . what did you say, that you're sick and tired of being mistreated? I don't know what you're talking about . . . that I created you just to make your life impossible throughout the entire plot? What plot are you talking about? This book doesn't even have a plot! In that precise instant, the parlor turns into a battlefield . . . spaceships fly over the roof . . . a mutant hamster destroys the wall . . . laser beams whistle everywhere, directional, coherent, monochromatic. As for the results of the confrontation, the climate could make the difference. Mandyjane remains hidden in the fog of cigarette smoke and coffee steam. If she were to crouch down a little maybe we could see her ass. She's sexy. With that demented adoration of herself, with the audacity of her crimes and with her cynicism in deception, Mandyjane pounces onto me and, with a ninja technique, ties up my wrists and ankles with ropes. The landscape is charred. I swear, you're wrong . . . what are you saying? that I've mistreated you because you're a female character? You are wrong again . . . I'm a feminist! The main character of my second novel was a woman! What, I made fun of her too? What's going on? Are you trying to censor me? Or something worse . . . . What do you want me to do, write books that everybody likes? I wouldn't do that even if I knew how! No one is ever honest enough. It's just words placed one after the other. Everything is conditioned by language. It makes communication become fresh and tidy. Alright, I get it: the author isn't always the master of the text. Giant antennae fall. Don't worry about the parts, observe the full picture. What did you say? You want me to get on my knees? Sure, fine, no problem. On the red carpet . . . ? Fine . . . like this? No? On all fours? What? You want me to lower my pants and underwear? OK . . . one moment, yeah, yeah, I'm doing it . . . what are you doing with that whip you just pulled out of your bag? Are you going to hit me? Ay! Punishment? For what? Oh, you are so unfair . . . Why do you treat me this way? This is all so humiliating and so . . . so exciting at the same time . . . you drive me wild . . . OK, hit me, hit me . . . ! Whip my ass

THE FAKE MUSE · 155

until it bleeds! . . . I'm your slave . . . yes, yes, yes, I'll do whatever you say . . . your wish is my command . . . go ahead, burn my nipples with that candle and then penetrate my anus until it tears and bleeds . . . What? you want me to say that I'm a pathetic phallocentric man who reproduces the patriarchal structures? Yes, I confess, I'm a pathetic, failed, disgusting old man . . . ! Everything I write is repulsive and sexist! I'm . . . what? You want me to shit myself and rub my face in my own excrement? But that's . . . that is disgusting . . . ! OK, OK, I'll do it . . . I'm your slave . . . your humble servant . . . I'll do it right now . . . I'm your slave, at your command . . . I'll rub my face into my own shit . . . like that, see? Yes, I'll let you dilate my anus to ram an enormous dildo in . . . rape me as much as you want, I can't say no . . . I'm your whore, your slave, sodomize me as you want if that is how I can make amends for all my mistakes . . . you are my mistress and I am your humble and humiliated slave, oh Queen of the Vampires, Goddess of Catastrophe . . . You want even more? What do you want me to do? You want me to ask for your forgiveness? Aha, you want me to ask for mercy, that's it . . . is there truly any difference between a fake muse and a real muse? You are so perverse, so incorruptible, so adorable . . . Very well, I swear that I will, I'll confess: forgive me. Forgive me for having come up with this whole absurd criminal fantasy filled with stupid violence. Forgive me for having objectified you and women and men and dogs and extraterrestrials . . . basically, everyone! I really believed that literature was the last free space to imagine and think whatever I felt like . . . but now I see that it's not . . . hit me . . . abuse me! . . . mistreat me! . . . I'll do whatever you say! . . . I'll do it . . . I'm your slave . . . your humble servant . . . I'll do it right now . . . I'm your slave, at your command . . . rape me as much as you want, I can't say no . . . I'm your whore, your slave, sodomize me all you want if that is how I can make amends for all my mistakes . . . you are my mistress and I am your humble and humiliated slave, oh Queen of the Vampires, Goddess of Catastrophe . . .

THE END

(Applause!!!!)
(Applause!!!!)
(Applause!!!!)

MAX BESORA has written five novels: *Volcano* (2011, rewritten and republished 2021), *The Marvelous Technique* (2014), *The Adventures and Misadventures of the Extraordinary and Admirable Joan Orpi, Conquistador and Founder of New Catalonia* (2017), *The Fake Muse* (2020), and *His Master's Voice* (2022), and one fictional essay on urban music, *Trapology* (2018).

MARA FAYE LETHEM is a writer, researcher, and literary translator. She has been recognized with a wide range of awards and nominations, including the National Book Critic Circle Gregg Barrios Award, the Prix Jan Michalski, and the Spain-USA Foundation Translation Award for her translation of Max Besora's *The Adventures and Misadventures of the Extraordinary and Admirable Joan Orpi, Conquistador and Founder of New Catalonia.*